Martini Club 4:
Rebellious: The 1920s
Perilous: The 1940s

by

Amanda McCabe

Martini Club 4: Rebellious and Perilous

Cover Art by *Lisa Dawn MacDonald*

The Wild Rose Press, Inc.
PO Box 708
Adams Basin, NY 14410-0708
Visit us at www.thewildrosepress.com

Publishing History
First Edition, 2021
Trade Paperback ISBN 978-1-5092-3760-9
Digital ISBN 978-1-5092-3761-6

Martini Club 4, Rebellious, Perilous

Published in the United States of America

REBELLIOUS...

Jessica studied his handsome face. With the smile gone, he looked older, harder. Haunted, even. Surely whatever he hid was far more dangerous than her own little secrets. But in that instant, the noise and the crowd faded around them, and she could only see him. He looked into her eyes, and she saw flash of raw pain there. Then it was hidden in another smile.

She knew then that, no matter what they each hid in their own hearts, he really saw her as no one else ever had. They were two of a kind. Risk takers. Curious. Wild.

It was exciting, new, wondrous—and it made her want to run away even as she never wanted to leave.

PERILOUS...

"Madeline," Christoph said solemnly as he started to hand her into the car. "Please, be most careful. Perhaps it would be best if you went back to London."

Maddie smiled up at him. "But I can't, not until after the graduation. Thank you for tea, Christoph, it was lovely. I hope we can talk again soon."

As the taxi sped away, she glanced out the back window to see him watching her go with a frown on his handsome face. Did he want to protect her, or was he hiding something? Either way, she was determined to find out, very soon.

The Martini Club 4 series consists of a total of eight stories by four different authors. They are intertwined and take place somewhat simultaneously, but they are best read in the following order:

Martini Club 4: The 1920s Stories:

Rebellious by Amanda McCabe
Ruined by Alicia Dean
Reckless by Kathy L Wheeler
Runaway by Krysta Scott

Martini Club 4: The 1940s Stories:

Pampered by Kathy L Wheeler
Priceless by Krysta Scott
Perilous by Amanda McCabe
Precarious by Alicia Dean

We hope you enjoy!

Martini Club 4: The 1920s

Rebellious

Prologue

England, 1924

"Such a lovely bride! The Hattons have certainly made a big production of this wedding, haven't they?"

"Wouldn't *you*, if you were them? Now they have one less hoydenish daughter to be rid of."

Lady Jessica Hatton choked on her forbidden cigarette as a laugh almost burst out of her at the two fusty old dowagers' words. Lady Briggsly and Mrs. Cartwright, the two biggest gossips around. They made it sound as if her parents had a whole tribe of flappers running loose in the ancient corridors of Hatton Hall. That sounded as if it would be quite fun, but alas there was only herself and her older sister Lulu, the newly disposed-of bride. And Lulu had never been at all hoydenish.

Jess, on the other hand...

Jessica slid down lower in her hiding place in the hollow of the huge old oak tree. The grove of trees was far beyond the huge white pavilions set up for Lulu and David Carlisle's wedding reception. She'd thought no one would venture away from the caviar and paté and all that free champagne. The sky was just turning pinkish at the edges as the sun sank lower, and the music was growing louder.

But nowhere was safe. Not at the Wedding Of The

Year, according to *Town Talk* magazine.

Jessica took another drag on her cigarette and prayed the guests would wander away soon.

"Well, Lady Louisa looked beautiful, I'll certainly give her that," one of the dowagers sniffed. "I heard they went to Paris to get the gown from Monsieur Poiret. As if Lucille of London wasn't grand enough."

"They had to distract everyone from the bridegroom, didn't they?" said her friend. "Poor man. He was so handsome once. I'm surprised Lady Louisa put back her veil to look at him."

Jessica nearly leaped out of her hidey-hole at those nasty words. David Carlisle was a war hero, once the best friend of their lost brother Bill, and the sweetest chap that ever lived! His scars only proved his bravery. If those old cows would just...

But then she remembered her mother's stern admonition before they climbed into the car to go to the church. *No scenes today, Jessica, I am warning you! No pranks at all. This is your sister's day.*

So Jess had once let a frog loose at the cake table at a wedding. That was ages ago when she was just a silly child, and it had been that snooty Millicent Haigh's reception anyway. She rather deserved the uproar.

But not Lulu and David. Their day had to be perfect, and it was. All clouds of tulle, orange blossoms, towering white cakes of spun sugar, and joyful smiles in two lives that had seen too much sadness. Jess would never do anything to mar that. Even now.

Yet she couldn't help but blow a ring of silvery smoke toward those old biddies.

"Do you smell something?" one of the ladies

shrieked. "Charlotte, you would never do such a thing as smoke would you?"

Jessica peeked out again to see that Lady Briggsly was holding her poor daughter, Charlotte Leighton, who had once been Jess's schoolfriend, by the hand. Charlotte looked miserable, as usual, and pale as a ghost in a silver chiffon dress.

"No, Mama," she muttered.

"These men and their vile cigarettes," Mrs. Cartwright said. "We should go back to the dancing."

"If only they hadn't hired a jazz band. So vulgar..."

Much to Jess's relief, they finally took poor Charlotte and wandered away and left her alone again. She stretched out her legs under the handkerchief hem of her pink satin Poiret bridesmaid's gown and settled in to enjoy her ciggie in peace.

Peace didn't last very long.

"There you are, you horrid thing!"

At the sound of that loud cry, Jess felt a rush of panic that her mother had found her. She tried to stub out the cigarette and whirled around, an excuse on her lips—only to find her best friend, Lady Margaret Montley, standing there.

Meggie's hands were planted on her hips as she gave Jess a mock glare. As usual, her wild golden curls were sliding from their jeweled combs, and her fashionably straight blue silk gown couldn't contain her unfashionably voluptuous figure. Meggie never cared at all that she wasn't in style; she was always unabashedly herself. It was the reason they had become immediate and fast pals at Mrs. Greensley's School For Young Ladies.

"Meggie, you gave me a heart seizure," Jess said.

"I thought you were Mum."

"She did look as if she was searching for you, but then David made her dance with him, so you're safe for a few minutes. I saw poor Charlotte Leighton being dragged away her mother. Here, scoot over so I can hide, too," Meggie said.

Jess slid over in the little hollow behind the tree and dug around in her beaded purse for her silver cigarette case and lighter. She lit up one for each of them, and they smoked in companionable silence for a long moment. The shadows of evening were creeping in, making the lights of the Chinese lanterns in the tents glow brighter, the music of the horns and the drums louder.

"Was that old Mrs. Cartwright I saw wandering away with Charlotte and her mother?" Meggie said.

"Mm-hm," Jessica answered. She tucked the short strands of her red-gold bob behind her ears. "She and her horrid old bosom bow. They were dreadful about David's scars."

"I doubt he would care one jot," Meggie said with a snort. "He and your sister looked heavenly happy. And we won't have to worry about the likes of them anymore either. Do you have it with you?"

Jessica laughed. "Of course I do! I carry it with me everywhere so I can remind myself it's almost time." She opened her purse again and found the tickets carefully folded and tucked in the bottom.

They each bent closer to read the precious words. The Cunard Line—*Empress of India*—departing Southampton for New York City. One first class cabin, two berths, for Jess and Meggie. Or rather, for their alter egos Miss Hampton and Mrs. Mortley.

"I can't believe it!" Meggie whispered in excitement. "Only a fortnight away."

"And then we'll be in New York!" Jess could hardly believe it herself. In only a few weeks, she would be away from England, away from her mother trying to force her into being the perfect deb, and wandering the glittering streets of New York. America. Sparkling high-rise windows, stretching all the way to the sky. Jazz, and shops, and taxis—and freedom.

"It will be even more fun than the time we put glue in the locks on finals day at Mrs. Greensley's. But are you sure they'll hire you once they see you're—well, not exactly what they're expecting?" Meggie said.

"Of course," Jess said with a confidence she didn't quite feel bone-deep. But she would have to make herself feel it, very soon. Confidence would carry her through. "They just want some plummy-sounding British aristocrat. A lady is as good as a lord when it comes to a byline. And I never *told* them I was a man."

She'd just signed her letter of application as JEO Hatton of Hatton Hall, Surrey. If they didn't think that meant Jessica Elizabeth Olivia Hatton, tough nuts to them. They'd liked her sample articles, and she would knock their socks off with what she could write there.

She was going to be a real, true-life newspaper writer. That was all that mattered.

"Come on," she said, putting out her cigarette. "Mum will be looking for us. We can't give her any cause for suspicion, not if we're going to pull this off."

"Oh, we'll pull it off all right," Meggie said with her usual confidence. "I'm not missing out on America for anything."

They hugged in a sudden burst of exuberant

giggles. It *was* going to happen! The adventure they had schemed and planned for ever since they were at school. It was finally coming true...

Chapter One

Aboard the Empress of India

"Do you smell that, Meggie?" Jessica cried as she leaned into the cold, salt spray wind, her T-strap shoes perched on the lowest rung of the ship's railing. She'd lost her hat, and the short strands of her hair blew into her eyes, but she didn't care. England was far behind them. They had escaped.

"It smells like freedom!" she shouted and threw up her arms. It felt like she could fly all the way to America.

"I only smell old fish," Meggie said. "Now come down from there, Jess. If you tumble into the drink, it will all be over before it even starts."

Jessica laughed and shook her head, but she did climb down. She spun around to see Meggie stretched out on one of the deck chairs, the glossy mink collar of her coat drawn close around her.

The sky *was* gray and dismal looking, the water not as glassy-smooth as when they slid past Ireland yesterday and headed out to open sea. Several of the passengers had retreated to their cabins, but Jessica couldn't stand staying inside. Not when there was so much to be seen.

"It smells like fish *and* freedom," Jessica insisted. "But we can go in now. Maybe Charlotte and Eliza will want to play some cards or mah-jong."

"Finally," Meggie grumbled as she swung her feet down to the damp deck. But her smile was broad. Jessica knew Meggie was loving it all just as much as she was.

"Come on, let's find Charlotte and Eliza," Jessica said, racing ahead toward the ship's salon. Their adventure had started growing on the boat train from London when they met their old schoolmate Charlotte Leighton and heard her romantic tale of fleeing an arranged marriage. So Victorian and tragic! They persuaded her to change her booking to their own ship.

And when they decided they should find a phony "lady's maid" to appear respectable and deflect suspicion, they found the perfect candidate on the docks in the person of Eliza Gilbert. A pretty ex-housemaid, she had been turned out of her position when her employer's evil son tried to seduce her.

Jessica made sure to take copious notes. If journalism didn't work out, surely she could turn to novel writing! The four of them were going to have to support themselves somehow. The running-away money she had saved for years wouldn't last much longer.

Meggie caught up with her, and hand in hand they ran toward the salon, laughing as they waved at some of the handsome sailors.

"Coming to the fancy dress party tonight, ladies?" one of them called.

"Wouldn't miss it for the world!" Jessica answered. Fancy dress parties were one of her very favorite things—and one at sea was bound to be doubly fun.

She swung around the corner, only to almost knock

over the lady standing outside the glass salon doors. They skidded on the slippery wooden deck, and Meggie had to grab both their arms to keep them from falling.

"I'm so sorry," Jessica gasped, dizzy. She saw it was the petite, delicate—and quite mysterious—Countess Markova she had almost barreled into. The lady was swathed in pale furs, a satin turban over her hair and a tiny white dog under her arm.

"*Nyet*," the countess said, waving a gloved hand. "Is—how you say? Nothing."

Jessica and Meggie exchanged a glance. The countess, obviously a Russian noblewoman cruelly cast out of her homeland by the Bolsheviks, had been an object of intense speculation for Jessica and her friends ever since they saw her come aboard. They all had ideas about what her dramatic story could be, but the lady herself was elusive. They only caught glimpses of her around the ship.

Like now. Jessica watched, fascinated, as the countess drifted away along the deck. At the railing, she took the arm of a tall man in a black overcoat and stylish black, broad-brimmed hat. He turned to smile down at her—and Jessica almost gasped.

It was quite shocking how good-looking he was. Surely men like that only existed in the cinema. Jessica was used to pale-faced, stammering boys from "good families" who steered her clumsily around the floor at tea dances and yammered on about cricket.

She would bet this man *never* talked about cricket. And that he could dance a wicked tango.

His profile under the brim of his hat was sharply cut, all elegant angles, his strong jaw roughened with whiskers as dark as his wavy black hair. Like a marble statue of some Roman god in a museum, only alive. Dark and vibrant.

Jessica shivered just looking at him.

"Good heavens! Do you suppose that's Ramon Novarro?" Meggie whispered, making Jessica break into giggles. They had just seen Novarro's movie *Thy Name is Woman* before they left England, and everyone had enormous crushes on him.

The countess and her stunning companion looked back at them at the sudden burst of noise. Jessica had a glimpse of wintery, sea-blue eyes, and suddenly she couldn't breathe. She felt so embarrassed, like a stupid little schoolgirl gawking at an actorly crush on the stage, yet neither could she turn away.

His smile widened as if he knew what she was thinking, and Jessica whirled around. She grabbed Meggie's arm and dragged her into the salon.

"I wasn't done staring," Meggie said with a laugh.

"I thought we were going to find the others and play mah-jong or something," Jessica snapped.

Meggie gave her a puzzled look, but she knew better than to say anything. She shrugged. "Sure. Sounds like fun. I'll grab a table, you go and find them."

Jessica spun around and rushed away, not quite sure where she was actually going. She just knew she *had* to get away from the glamorous countess's companion before she dissolved into a puddle of blushes and giggles, like all those silly girls she and Meggie went to Mrs. Greensley's School with, and who she wanted to forget. She was starting a brand-new, grown-up life in a new city, no more silly English missishness!

She ran up a narrow flight of stairs, rolling slightly with the waves of the ship, and along a corridor. Two passing sailors called out cheerful greetings as she hurried past.

"Still coming to the fancy dress party?" one said, as did everyone who had seen her that day. The party was all she could think about until she saw the countess's matinee idol friend.

"Of course," she answered with a laugh. "I'm counting on you for my costume, don't forget."

"How could we forget *that*?" the sailor said with a wink, making her laugh even harder. He was handsome, with blond curls and broad shoulders, and like all his mates was fun company to play cards and shuffleboard with on the long voyage. Yet when he teased her, flirted with her, it didn't make her even a fraction as flustered as one look from "Ramon Novarro."

She gave the sailors a jaunty wave and hurried on to the cabin she and Meggie now shared with Eliza and Charli at the end of the corridor. She had to shove hard at the door since someone's hatbox was in the way, and inside the same scene of chaos she'd left a few hours ago greeted her.

The four narrow bunks were unmade and strewn with dresses and silky slips and combinations, with shoes shoved underneath haphazardly. Pots of lotions and tubes of lipsticks were scattered across the one table bolted beneath the small porthole.

In the meager, grayish light that came in through the thick glass, Jessica saw that Charli hadn't left her bunk. She was huddled underneath her blankets, her nose buried in a book. Her carrot-red hair, brighter than Jessica's strawberry, which they had persuaded her to

11

bob with Eliza's sewing scissors, was tousled, her spectacles perched on the end of her nose.

Eliza stood at the small basin, rinsing out a shirtwaist. The smell of Persil soap, flowery and rich, hung in the stuffy air.

"Eliza, we told you—no more washing up! You aren't really our maid." Jessica stamped across the cabin to tug the blankets off Charlotte's knees. "It's a lovely day outside. Come up on deck and play mah-jong with us."

"Horsefeathers! I just need to get out this one spot..." Eliza muttered.

"And I need to finish this chapter!" Charli argued.

"No, and no." The cabin was so small Jessica could snatch away both the wet shirtwaist and the book with only two steps. "It's time for fun now. Come on!"

Charli still tried to protest, fun being so new to her, but Eliza got into the spirit of things and caught the book from Jessica's hand to keep it away from her.

"Mah-jong, and no more arguments!" Jessica cried, twirling away. "In half an hour, in the salon."

Before anyone could make another protest, she skipped out into the corridor and slammed the cabin door behind her. The narrow hallways were deserted now, all the crew off on their duties and all the passengers resting up for the fancy dress party. All that silence, the roll of the carpeted floor beneath her feet, the faint, far-away roar of the ship's engines, made her feel restless again. Giddy. She took off running, leaping up the stairs in exactly the way her mother had always scolded her not to.

She swung around a corner—and almost tripped to a sudden standstill. The devastatingly handsome man she saw with the countess earlier stood near the railing, talking with another man, one in the uniform of a crew's officer.

There was nothing wrong with that, of course. Jessica talked to the ship's crew all the time. But she didn't know this officer at all, and something about *that* man, the matinee idol in all his silver-screenish glory, made her freeze in her headlong dash. She slowly backed up and ducked around the corner before they could spot her.

She carefully peeked at them, wishing she could hear what they were saying. The crew member had his back to her, but she could see the handsome stranger's profile under the brim of his hat. There was a darkly intent look on his chiseled features, a tautness that almost looked like barely leashed—anger. His hand, with its long, elegant fingers, was curled into a fist on the railing.

One of the reasons Jessica wanted to be a reporter so badly was the simple fact that people were so fascinating, and so—so *weird*. Ever since she was a kid, she carried around a notebook to jot down things people said or did that she could puzzle over and decipher later. She loved hearing people's stories, discovering their secrets.

And she would bet that "Ramon Novarro" over there had a doozy.

She stared, watching as the two men went on talking in low, barely coherent voices, words that were snatched away on the sea breeze. Their glances between themselves were not what she would call friendly, either. What could be going on there?

Jeepers, but she wished she had her notebook with

her!

Just as her neck was starting to get sore from craning around the corner, the crew member gave an abrupt nod and stalked away. She had a quick glimpse of his craggy, bearded face as he passed her hidey-hole, and he definitely looked angry. Angry and, astonishingly, scared. Scared of what? Her mind raced with all sorts of wonderfully lurid possibilities. Gambling debts. Rum-running. Blackmail. Quarrels over a beautiful showgirl.

No, not a showgirl. Not for "Ramon Novarro," surely. She didn't like that thought at all.

"You can come out from there now, if you like. It can't be very comfortable pressed up to the wall like that," the matinee idol suddenly said. He spoke quietly, calmly, but his faintly accented voice carried to her all too well on the salty wind. He sounded amused.

To her shame, she felt a hot blush flare across her face to be caught eavesdropping like that, and by *him* of all people. But really, who was he to make her feel like a chastened child about to be sent to bed with no supper? She was Lady Jessica Hatton, daughter of an earl, and a soon-to-be famous reporter, too.

She stood up so ramrod-straight her old deportment teacher at Mrs. Greensley's would be proud, tossed her head back, and marched out of her hiding place. He glanced over his shoulder at her, and she saw that the corners of his mouth looked as if he was just about to smile, but other than that he didn't look as if he moved at all.

And up-close she saw he was even more breathtakingly handsome. The real Ramon Novarro should worry about losing his job to pale blue eyes and cheekbones that could cut glass.

"I didn't want to interrupt what looked like a private conversation," she said haughtily, trying to mimic her mother's best "countess" tone. She felt totally ridiculous, though.

What was it about this man that made her feel so wrong-footed? All those debutante balls, tea dances, even curtsying to the queen, should have knocked shyness out of her.

He turned to fully face her, and that tiny, secret smile turned into a full-blown grin that almost knocked her back a step it was so gorgeous.

"I should go," she said, the "countess" voice totally gone. "My friends are waiting."

She spun around, away from the sight of him, but it was no good. She could still feel him watching her with those pale, sea-colored eyes. That smile.

"Are you coming to the dance tonight?" he called, and she suddenly recognized that accent. It sounded Russian, like all the refugees from the Revolution who had flooded into London's ballrooms in the last couple of years. That only made him even more intriguing, damn him.

"I shall have to check my calendar. It is rather full at the moment," she said airily, rather proud of how calm she sounded now.

He ruined all that by laughing. *Laughing!* Even worse, his laughter sounded delicious, like the slide of a first sip of fizzy champagne.

She dashed away, but even as she ducked into the salon like it was her last sanctuary, closing her eyes against the day, she could still hear that laughter in her mind. That accent...

"Jeepers, Jess, but what happened to you?" Meggie cried. "You look like a ghost chased you down the deck."

Jessica opened her eyes to see her friends were all gathered around the table already, the mah-jong tiles spread in front of them. They all stared up at her curiously, Charli squinting a little without her specs.

Flustered, Jessica pushed herself away from the door and shook her skirt back into place. She would probably tell them all about the Russian matinee idol, but not now. Tonight, in their cabin, when it was dark and she didn't feel so horribly shaken-up. When she could think rationally about the mystery of him.

For now, though, he was just her little secret.

"I just took a wrong turn belowdecks and got lost," she said with a laugh. "Come on, are we playing mah-jong or not?"

****

Durak! Nicolai Dimitriovich Romanov-Markov, now known by everyone as Frank Markov, watched the red-headed sprite of a girl dash away like a bright butterfly in the gray day. He had seen her before, standing on the ship's railing with her arms flung out as if she would fly and racing around the decks laughing with her friends. It had made him laugh, too, just to see the sheer, raw exuberance of her. Had he ever been that young? He didn't think so anymore.

And it had been far too long since he laughed at anything at all.

Frank turned away from the sight of her and rubbed his hand hard over the back of his neck as he muttered another curse. With her bright hair and vivid spirit, she reminded him too much of another such shining spirit.

A girl who once spun through the gilded ballrooms of St. Petersburg, drawing him out onto palm-shielded verandas with her laughter and the scent of gardenias in her hair. Before she sent him off to war with just such a flower pressed into his hand.

But that girl was long-gone now, along with all of his old life in Russia. He couldn't afford to lose himself in this woman's radiance, no matter how deeply tempted he was to run after her now. To demand to know her name, to make her tell him what she laughed at. She was obviously a lady, with her fine accent and manners, despite her bobbed hair and free laughter.

He had a mission now, and where he was going no one could follow. Especially not aristocratic butterfly girls like that redhead.

"Did you speak to him?" someone said suddenly in Russian.

Frank turned to see his aunt, the Countess Markova as she was now known, standing at the railing behind him. That she had been able to creep up on him like that was another bad sign of his distraction. Her beautiful face smiled, but he saw the hardness behind it.

"He will do it," Frank answered in the same language. In that instant of coming face-to-face with the laughing girl, he'd almost forgotten why they were on the *Empress of India* in the first place. The mission that had taken them from Siberia to Paris and London, and now to New York, where they would finally end things. Finally have their revenge.

He wouldn't forget again.

A brittle smile curved the countess's pretty, pink-rouged mouth, but her ice-blue eyes were flat and opaque. "Excellent. The more allies we can find the better."

"Allies? Or mere greedy minions?" he said with a bark of humorless laughter.

"Does it matter? As long as they are useful to us." She took a step closer to him and laid her gloved hand on his arm. Her touch was light, but in it he felt all the iron weight of their past. The blood-stained snow. The screams.

"You have surely not lost your resolve?" she said.

"*Nyet*," he answered brusquely. "I will never forget. You know that."

"Good. Not when we are so close to the end."

She tugged at his arm, and he let her lead him toward the smoking salon. She was right. The end, which they had schemed and plotted and killed for, was finally within sight. He would never give it up for anything. He had vowed that to his lost family.

But he couldn't help one glance back, just to see if there was still one last glimpse of strawberry-red hair. But she was gone.

Chapter Two

"I feel so melancholy since cutie went away! I know it's folly that makes me feel this way. Oh, I feel like Romeo once fell for Juliet, I've got that wild lovin' that you never will forget...'"

Jessica could hear the music before she even reached the open doors of the ship's grand ballroom. It swept down the wide, carpeted corridor like a twist of sparkling sun, the sound of pure joy and happiness on the rumble of dancing feet.

She spun around herself, laughing. It was always that way when Meggie sang. Her voice didn't seem to match her exuberant, blonde-ringleted self. It was a dark, low, throaty velvet, as rich and delicious as chocolate cake, and it always made everyone around long to either dance or sob with raw emotion.

Jessica twirled to a stop just outside the doors and caught a glimpse of herself in one of the wall-length, gilt-framed mirrors. Eliza's magical needle had done its work on the sailor's white, baggy uniform, and now the linen trousers and tunic fit her slim figure like a glove. The taken-up hem revealed her silver sequined dance shoes, the only part of the costume not nautically approved. The white hat sat perched on her bobbed hair.

She tilted it to a jaunty angle and slipped into the crowded ballroom.

Meggie stood onstage in her absolute element. The spotlight gathered and caught on her, shining on the silver satin Eliza had made into a goddess's toga. Her blonde curls were twisted up with glittering strands of tinsel, but it didn't sparkle as much as her smile as she held up her arms and sang. In the shadows behind her, the ship's band played the song, *Wild Romantic Blues*, their instruments flashing in the darkness.

Jessica stayed to the edge of the room for the moment, studying the crowd as if she was writing a scene. This was the best part of any party, gauging the atmosphere, the mix of people. This one wasn't too crazy yet. Couples spun around the checkered, lighted floor in a foxtrot to Meggie's song, a blur of satin and velvet costumes, swaying fringe and sparkling beads. But there seemed to be a hum in the air of anticipation, a burst of fun just barely held in check.

Jessica caught a glass of champagne from the tray of a waiter passing by and slowly circled the dance floor. Along the carved gilt walls were long, white damask-draped buffet tables covered with tiered trays of smoked salmon, caviar on blinis, stuffed mushrooms, lobster patties, and luscious, glossy French chocolates, all watched over by an enormous ice sculpture of Poseidon with his trident.

Besides the glasses of champagne, a bartender was busy mixing up sidecars and pink ladies, their bright colors almost luminous in gloved hands. High above her head, fairy lights glowed from the coffered ceiling. It was all as grand and elaborate as any London debutante ball her sister Lulu's friends would host.

And it was just like what she was trying to get away from by running to New York. But there was something in the air that night on the sea, something sparkling and reckless that made her feel like being wild, too. Like taking a chance on something, anything new.

Her glass of champagne was empty, and she glimpsed a pyramid of full glasses on the buffet table. She gave a waiter her empty one and reached for another, but just as her hand stretched out someone reached out in front of her. Someone with long, elegant, sun-bronzed fingers and an impeccable French cuff fastened with ebony studs.

Jessica realized with a hot-cold thrill that she remembered those very hands resting on the polished deck railing earlier.

"For you, mademoiselle?" he said, offering her the glass. She could hear the smile in his voice, in that light, lilting accent.

The champagne, so fizzy and golden-delicious, gulped down so fast, had already gone to her head a bit. She felt dizzy and a little silly. Or maybe that was just *him* making her feel that way.

She turned and looked up into his eyes, so blue they didn't seem real. His hair was brushed back in a glossy wave from his sharply sculpted face, and she saw that there was actually a cleft in his square-cut jaw. She giggled as she realized she wanted more than anything to press her fingertip just there. Deep enough for a girl to fall in and swim in it.

She knew she shouldn't do it, but something made her take the glass from his beautiful hand and gulp down another sip.

"Somehow I don't think you're French, monsieur," she said.

He laughed, and it sounded startled, almost rusty, as if he very seldom laughed. "No," he said, a hint of that intriguing laughter still in his voice. "I am not French. But tonight everyone is what they want to be, yes?"

That *was* why Jessica always loved a masquerade ball. The chance to cover up real life in all sorts of disguises, to slip away just for a few hours and try something else.

He was right. Tonight was about being whatever she wanted, and just like that her mind was made up. "Yes," she said with a decisiveness she was far from feeling. She drank down the last of her champagne and put down the empty glass. "And what I want right now is a dance."

He glanced past her to the dance floor, the stage. Meggie had left, and now the band played a quickstep. That was a dance she loved, so full of life and fun. It made her feel bold all over again, bold and scared and excited all at the same time, and she knew that was the kind of life she was seeking.

"Very well," he said, giving her a low, old-world kind of bow. "Would you honor me with a dance, then, mademoiselle?"

In answer, Jessica stepped closer to him and slid one hand over his shoulder, taking the other lightly against her palm. He was taller than she, hard and warm under her hands, and she felt the smooth fineness of his wool evening coat. He was stronger and broader than any of her London Etonian dance partners.

He moved with her into the flow of the other dancers willingly enough, but his body felt stiff against hers, as if he held himself cautiously. Jessica impulsively tugged him closer and was rewarded with one of those glorious laughs. She laughed, too, even though her heart was pounding so loudly in her ears she could hardly hear the music. Only years and years of dance lessons kept her moving in the right pattern, feet to the left, feet to the right, spin around, skip.

That, and the fact that her mysterious matinee idol partner was a sublime dancer. He led her so easily, so gracefully, she barely had to think of where to move next.

Jessica rested her cheek on his shoulder and closed her eyes just to feel that one moment. The music swayed, quick, quick, slow, and she let the tune wind around her just like the warmth of his hand at her back, his strong body.

He was such an intriguing stranger. She spent her life in stories, writing them, reading them, dreaming them up, and she had never wanted to know a story more than she wanted to know his.

Their steps slid together perfectly, their two bodies fitting as if they had always been just like that. She'd never had a dance like that. She never wanted it to end, but of course it had to. Just like everything else that was glorious.

As the song wound to a close, his arms slipped away from her, and he took a step back. For a second, Jessica swayed, afraid her legs wouldn't hold her up anymore. She shook away the shimmering clouds of that dream-dance and blinked up at him. He looked back at her with a strange, wry smile on his sensual lips. She couldn't read it at all.

"Thank you for the dance, mademoiselle," he said. "It was most—memorable."

Memorable? He gave her another of those old-fashioned, courtly bows and turned to vanish into the sparkling crowd.

For a long moment, Jessica couldn't move at all. Had she just dreamed that whole thing, dreamed *him*? She pushed her way past the people who pressed in around her, straining up on her tiptoes, trying to catch another glimpse of him. But he was gone.

Just like a dream indeed, popping like a shimmering bubble on waking.

"Blast it all," she muttered.

"Jess? Are you okay?"

Jessica spun around to see Charlotte watching her. Charli wore a Cleopatra costume, soft folds of white drapery bound with a gold sash, gold sandals, and a headdress of blue and red beads. She had left her specs behind, but her wide eyes were still much too perceptive.

"Nothing at all!" Jessica cried. She sounded too brittle-bright, even to her own ears. She snatched up two fresh glasses of champers and thrust one into Charlotte's hand. "Here's to the future, then," she said in a jaunty toast. "May nothing get in our way..."

Chapter Three

New York City, six months later

"Mrs. Astor's garden party?" Jessica gasped as she looked down at the papers that had just been slapped down on her desk.

"To benefit the Women's Aid Society, of course," Mrs. Perkins, the head of the Society Pages at the *New York World*, sniffed. She peered down her long, sharp nose at Jessica with that smugly satisfied gleam in her beady eyes. It always made Jessica want to give her a swipe just to see what would happen. "It is one of the most important social events in New York this month, the beginning of the autumn season. Mrs. Astor loves to show off her famous greenhouses. I am not at all sure you are up to the challenge, *Lady* Jessica, but Mr. Thorpe says your byline would look, and I quote, peachy."

With one more sniff, Mrs. Perkins spun around and marched off in a flash of upswept white hair and black silk skirts. The click of her low heels on the linoleum floor blended with the clack of the typewriters.

Jessica slumped back in her chair and resisted the urge to stick out her tongue at Mrs. Perkins's black-clad back. A garden party—after last week's tea at the Plaza Hotel, and the tennis club meeting the week before that, and the display of new Paris hats before that. Not to mention the dog show, where Mrs. Stuyvesant's Chow-

Chow took first place.

"If I wanted to write about drivel like that, I would have stayed in London," she muttered. "So beastly."

She slowly reached for a pencil and the paper with her new assignment. Was it really only a few months ago she had stepped onto the elevator here at the *World*, a portfolio of story ideas under her arm and joy bursting in her heart at the thought of bringing real, important, life-changing news into peoples' lives? Things like the upcoming American election, or even the first Macy's Thanksgiving parade. She wanted to make a difference with the only thing she was good at, the only thing that made her stand out—her pen. Her words.

"What a chump I was," she whispered. She glanced toward the closed door of Mr. Thorpe, the editor's office, and she *did* stick out her tongue at that. Just a little. He'd been shocked she was a female that first day, just as Meggie had warned her. But only at first. Then a smile she didn't like at all crossed his jowly, reddened face, and he rubbed his ink-stained fingers together. An earl's daughter's name *was* useful—but not for covering crime and corruption. "No one cares about that rubbish anyway," he'd said.

She was useful for covering garden parties and dog shows. Impressing society sorts.

Jessica sharpened her pencil with far more ferocity than the innocent stick of wood deserved. She'd come to New York so full of silly hopes, silly confidence that she could *make* things happen, when she could have stayed in London and done much the same thing. Wrote adorable little descriptions of flower arrangements and ladies' hats for some fribble of a paper. Her parents would have let her write stuff like that—for a while. As an amusement. Until she picked one of her cricket-playing, country house owning dance partners to properly marry.

No way that was going to happen. She hadn't come so far just to stay the same. Her family would surely come after her soon enough, but she had some time to make a difference.

She sharpened another pencil and glanced out the window beyond the sea of desks. Gleaming, silvery buildings towered against a gray sky, pulsing with sheer, raw new life behind every window. A plane wheeled over the river, light as a feather as it soared over the diamond-sharp spires of the skyscrapers and then soared away into the clouds.

That was why she had come to New York, to be a part of that life, of all those stories that were so different from what she left behind.

New York was just like those new jazzy songs Meggie sang. You never knew what direction it was going to veer off in, where the tale was going to go. At home, every day, every year, was the same, all laid out for her in a predictable pattern before she was even born. Here—anything at all could happen. She could *make* it happen.

She just had to write about garden parties first.

She turned to see Miss Jones, the woman at the next desk, giving her a wry smile. Miss Jones had been at the *World* for years, writing about the very same topics. There was a blandness in her faded blue eyes, a coolness about the way she watched everything, as if she had seen it all before and wasn't much impressed.

But Jessica enjoyed her dry little jokes, they made the boring days move along a little faster. She'd been very helpful showing Jessica some of the office ropes.

"The Astor garden party, then?" Miss Jones said.

Jessica nodded. "I'm not sure how many ways to describe pink hydrangeas. Dusty rose, mauve, mulberry-tipped, burgundy..."

"Fuchsia, heliotrope." Miss Jones laughed. "Yes, I know the challenge. You'll get used to it."

Jessica sighed. That was the problem. She was already "used to it"—she'd been living it her whole life. She wanted something new. Different. Exciting.

For a second, an image flashed through her mind of the masked ball on the ship. The music, the champagne—a pair of jewel-blue eyes looking at her as they danced so perfectly together. *That* had been exciting. But she'd never seen him again, not even on the ship.

Jessica pushed away the memory, a memory that came into her head much too often when she couldn't sleep at night, and gritted her teeth. She reached for her pencil to make some notes on Mrs. Astor and her blasted garden party, but a restlessness had seized her. She couldn't come up with any new words for pink at all.

She pushed herself away from her desk and hurried out of the crowded office. Maybe a walk would help. She passed the packs of girls bent over their clacking typewriters, the typing pool Meggie had been fired from after less than a week, mainly because she couldn't really type or get up so early in the morning. Jessica turned away from Mr. Thorpe's office door, the window of it clouded with old, yellowing cigarette smoke. At the end of the room, a cluster of young, eager cub reporters gathered around a table.

"...the Bolshies are hiding there, my source in the police department just knows it," she heard. Just enticing little snatches, hints of a world of important stories far beyond hats and dog shows. They got quieter as she passed, their eyes following her with a look of mingled suspicion and admiration. She wouldn't get anything interesting out of them, even if she flirted and tried to take advantage of the admiration side of that coin. They wouldn't tell her what the "Bolshies" or the police were after now.

She strode past them, out the double glass doors of the paper, and impatiently pressed the button for the lift. No, not a lift, not in America—the *elevator*. She needed some fresh air.

Before it could arrive, the doors behind her opened again, and Paul Hindley tumbled out. Tall, red-headed, loose-limbed to the point of clumsiness, his tie always crooked. Jessica sighed and made herself smile at him. He'd taken to hanging around her desk too much lately, chattering about baseball and the gin joints he frequented. She sensed he was somehow winding up to ask her out sometime, and while he was surely nice enough, he was too much like those boys at home, with their cricket and their tea dances.

There was no mystery about Paul, no intrigue. No sky-blue eyes or Russian accents.

"Hi, Paul," she said. "I was just going to pop out for a quick walk."

"Oh, that sounds peachy-keen," he said eagerly. "Maybe I could go with you? Or..." He glanced back toward the glass doors where his fellow reporter cronies watched him closely. "Or maybe not now, I guess. Dinner sometime? I know a great Italian joint just around the corner."

Jessica considered it for a moment. After a few glasses of illicit Chianti, maybe he would be willing to drop her a hint about the Bolshie story. But she immediately felt guilty for the thought of using him like that. Paul was a nice enough bloke, in his own way. She would just have to find her own way to figure that one out.

The elevator arrived at last, and Jessica gratefully stepped into it. When she turned, Paul was watching her, his eyes wide with hope. She waved at him, but she didn't actually see him. "Can't this week, awfully busy!" she called brightly. "Maybe later?"

"Anytime," he said sadly as the doors slid closed between them.

Poor Paul. But he *had* given her the spark of an idea, and she couldn't believe it never occurred to her before.

She just had to find her own story. No editor was going to just walk out and give it to her, not when they could just pat her on the head and send her off to flower shows. But if she found a gonzo story, some breaking news no one else knew about...

They would have to pay attention then.

She almost laughed aloud and clapped her hand over her mouth so the elevator operator wouldn't think she was going bananas. She'd run away from home by herself; surely she could dig up a story by herself. But where to start?

****

"I think that's the last of it, boss."

Frank Markov looked up from the inventory list on the bar as Yevgeny heaved a crate on top of the pyramid that was already there, ready to be unpacked and turned into cocktails. They were all marked "Lemon Juice" and "Apples—Vermont," but gave off the unmistakable clink of glass. Yevgeny, who had once been Frank's sergeant in the long-ago nightmare days of the war and now helped with any strong-arming that needed to be done, gave a satisfied grin.

"We're ready to open soon, *da*?" Yevgeny said.

Frank studied the room around them. Club 501 had once been the best speakeasy in town, until the old owner ran afoul of his suppliers and had to sell out in a hurry. The all-new, refurbished club was meant to be the swankiest, most luxurious, most exclusive club in New York, and every detail was perfected toward that aim. Everything was gilded and marble, sparkling and shimmering. Like something in his old life, in the old Russia.

His aunt, with her exquisite taste honed in the royal palaces of St. Petersburg, had chosen the furnishings and rich draperies, the dark red and burnished gold that made everything feel rich and intimate.

Frank had been in charge of ordering the liquor, organizing the men. There was no bathtub hooch or blinding moonshine, only the best wine from France, brandies and ports from England, whisky from Scotland, brought down from Canada with secret help from the governor himself. Though no one could really know that. As far as the patrons and most employees of Club 501 knew, they were just another speakeasy, albeit a very fine and exclusive one. Word of its wonders had been spread around until now everyone who was anyone in New York wanted to be there.

For their carefully constructed scheme to work,

that secret had to hold. There could be no mistakes now, no false steps. It had taken many months of making the right contacts in Paris and London, bringing the New York politicians and police into the scheme of using bootlegging and a popular speakeasy to corral the Bolsheviks trying to infiltrate the United States. Everything had to be right.

His family, lost in the upheaval of Russia, deserved some justice now.

Frank ran his hand over the cool marble of the bar. "We'll open very soon indeed, Yevgeny. It's all in place."

Yevgeny's scarred, Slavic-sculpted face hardened, and he brought a meaty fist down on a crate. The precious glass rattled. "They will all pay now."

Frank frowned. *They will pay*—that was what he'd been working toward for so very long. Every calculated move he made, every deal he cemented, it was all to revenge his lovely mother and their lost home. The evildoers who killed her and tore his whole country apart. It was all coming to bitter fruition soon. But he had the hard, weary certainty that this was only the beginning. That his whole life would be spent burning up in anger over the past.

Suddenly, an image of the girl from the ship flashed through his mind. Her shining eyes, her bright eagerness, the way she made things seem so sunny-brilliant for a moment.

But a girl like that was beyond him now. He had seen too much ugliness, done too much, to deserve brightness like that. His course was set a long time ago.

"Come, Yevgeny," he said. "We have work to do if this place is going to open on time."

Chapter Four

"Jess! Oh, you will never guess what's happened, not in a million, trillion years!"

Jessica laughed as Meggie grabbed her hands as soon as she stepped into the flat at The Gables boardinghouse, spinning her around in a circle. She still felt windblown and jostled from the crowded streets, and her straw cloche hat went flying, but she still had to laugh. Meggie's excitement was contagious, and it built on her own until they were both shouting with it. Meggie let go of her, and they toppled onto the old, sagging sofa.

Jessica picked up her hat from the floor, and shook off her pinching, T-strap shoes. She almost needed to buy new stockings, and she didn't want to rub any more holes in the thin silk. She glanced around the small room with its peeling wallpaper and rickety old kitchen table, the single sink piled with dishes. It was quiet for late afternoon; she wondered where the others could be.

"It's true," she gasped. "I'll never guess. What's up?"

Meggie bounced up and down on the sofa, clapping her hands as the old springs squeaked like they were dying. "I got a new job! Isn't that wonderful?"

"Oh, Meggie," Jessica groaned. Meggie's jobs—in the typing pool at the paper, the front desk of a hotel, waitressing at a tea room—had come and gone like sparkling Chinese lanterns tossed around in the wind, in between auditions at every music hall she could find. The ten dollar weekly rent on their two rooms on the fifth floor, with the sink in the entryway and the kitchen down the hall, always managed to get paid, but she wanted Meggie to find something she loved to do. "What is it? Waitress again? Remember what happened when you spilled tea on that Texas oilman's wife. Or salesgirl at Bloomingdale's?"

"No, silly! I knew waitressing wasn't for me after that ridiculous cow screamed down the tea room. I did her a favor, ruining that horrible skirt. But this is a *real* job. Sort of. At least I'll get paid for it, cash, every night. And I'll be *singing*!"

"Really?" Jessica cried in excitement. "One of your auditions paid off?"

Meggie bit her lip and glanced away. "Well—it's not exactly Broadway. Not yet. But who knows what could happen? I could meet lots of famous people now. Directors, theater owners, film stars..."

Some of that excitement cooled off into suspicion. "Where is this job, then?"

"Club 501! I'll be singing there. Solo, with a proper band and everything. Oh, Jess, isn't it lovely?"

Club 501! Jessica gasped. Everyone knew about Club 501, it was one of the newest, most exclusive, most fun speakeasies in town. Or it soon would be, once it opened. Spoken of in whispers at the newspaper and in the shops, nothing like the bar in the basement of their apartment building where Jess and Meggie sometimes stopped for a quick orange blossom.

Club 501 was said to be so elegant, all velvet and gilt, with the best cuisine and real booze brought from

Canada and shipped up from the West Indies, mixed up by real bartenders. Populated by people just like the ones Meggie said—theater owners and their beautiful actress mistresses, film stars, foreign royalty. And now Meggie had a job there!

Surely this was a sign that Jessica's new story was also right around the corner. Maybe even at the famous Club 501.

"How did you get this job?" Jessica said. "Tell me all about it!"

"It was easy, really," Meggie said, her eyes still sparkling. "I met a couple of girls at my audition yesterday, some twins who have a dancing act. None of us got callbacks on that show, but they told me they were headed to Club 501, that some famous writer guy they met at a party set it up for them. They let me tag along, and we all got hired!"

"And did you actually see the place? What's it like?"

Meggie flopped back onto the sofa with a dramatic sigh. "It's *gorgeous*, Jess! Even better than they say. Though it was dark during the day, of course, so I couldn't make out all the details, but they had velvet banquettes, a big dance floor, a marble bar, paintings on the walls—one was a Monet, I'm sure. It was practically empty when I went there, but I can see how swell it will be at night."

"When do you start?"

"Tomorrow. The band's singer eloped last week, lucky for me. You'll come, won't you, Jess? I won't be nearly so nervous to start if you're there."

Jessica laughed. Meggie was never nervous once she started singing. "You would have to pay me to stay away, Megs. I'm dying for a peek at that place."

Meggie's smile suddenly faded, and she plucked at the faded cushion of the sofa. "There is one more thing..."

Jessica wasn't sure she could handle "one more thing." The day had already been jam-packed with revelations. "What? Charli is marrying the Prince of Wales?"

"Better! You will never guess who runs Club 501."

A story already? No one in New York knew who ran the place, he was said to be just as elegant and mysterious as his club. If she could find out the mystery man's identity...

"William Randolph Hearst? Douglas Fairbanks?" Jessica teased.

Meggie snorted. "You will never guess in a decade! It's the man from the ship. The one with the movie star looks, but better than Fairbanks, I think. The one who was friends with the countess. *He* runs Club 501. Isn't that astonishing?"

Astonishing didn't go far enough. Jessica was completely gobsmacked. She stared at Meggie, afraid her jaw was sagging.

The blue-eyed Russian—*her* blue-eyed Russian, as she sometimes thought of him secretly at night? The man she had once danced with, all too briefly? She'd been so sure she would never see him again, and Megs was saying he was practically right around the corner. Running a nightclub.

Jessica shook her head. Doing inventory of crates of bottles and keeping an eye on bartenders and wait staff, hiring singers and bribing the police, didn't seem like the right job for him. Running a speakeasy was no walk in the park, she knew that well enough, but still—it didn't seem dark and dangerous enough for him, with his pale eyes full of secrets and his musical accent.

She sat back, trying to hide the strength of her reaction. She didn't know what to say about him, even to Meggie. "You met him at your audition?"

"Yes, but he didn't say much. Just asked me what I was going to sing, whispered something to the piano player, said 'thanks very much.' It was the piano player who said I was hired. He didn't mention the ship." Meggie gave her a sly, teasing smile. "I knew that would make you come to my debut for sure!"

Jessica laughed. "Wild horses couldn't drag me away anyway. But I admit, he was—interesting."

"He's definitely that. So gorgeous. And that voice!" Meggie gave another dramatic sigh. "But he didn't look twice at me, even though I was wearing my new silver dress."

There was the rattle of keys in the hallway, and the door swung open. Eliza stepped in, her face pale, as it had been too often lately. The job at the factory seemed to be making her ill. That worried expression vanished when she saw them sitting there, and she flashed a smile. Jessica knew if they tried to confront her again, tried to pester her with questions about what was going on, she would just evade them once more. But Jess was determined to find out, to help if she could. And she was nothing if not persistent.

"What are you two doing home early?" Eliza said cheerfully. She carefully stowed her threadbare purse behind the kitchen table, which was already piled with neglected mail, worn-out dancing shoes, and theater programs.

"Meggie got a proper sort of job," Jessica said. "And you will never guess where!"

"The Shubert Theater?" Eliza said, laughing as she got into the spirit. "Or running The Plaza?"

"Better!" Meggie said. "I'm going to be singing at Club 501. And you're all invited to the front row at my debut tomorrow night."

To Jessica's shock, Eliza's face turned milk white. She swayed on her worn-heeled shoes, but before Jessica and Meggie could reach for her, she grabbed onto the back of the sofa, and her expression went completely blank.

"Club 501?" she whispered. "The speakeasy?"

"Yes," Meggie said uncertainly, shooting Jessica a glance. "Is something wrong, Eliza?"

Eliza shook her head. "Just haven't eaten today, I guess. Tell me about your new job, then, Megs. How did you get it? Who did you talk to?"

Jessica and Meggie exchanged puzzled looks, but there was no time to talk about it now. Jessica gave her a tiny shrug and mouthed *Later*. Meggie nodded.

"I just heard the band needed a new singer, thanks to these girls at an audition..." Meggie began.

Chapter Five

"It doesn't look like much from out here, does it?" Charli said.

Jessica glanced back at Charli, studying her in the faint, phosphorescent orange glow from the streetlight on the corner. Charli frowned doubtfully at the row of plain, almost factory-looking buildings lined up in front of them on the alleyway off Broadway. She clutched the front of her coat closed, but other than that she didn't look much like the shy, shrinking girl Jessica and Meggie had teased at Mrs. Greensley's school. Her hair was cut in a fashionable wedge now, her glasses left behind. She had definitely been coming out of her shell under the influence of New York.

Jessica turned back to look at the building. The windows stared down at them in blank darkness, and she could only hear the faint roar of traffic from Broadway, a woman's shrill laughter, a cat howling from behind a trash can.

"No, not from here," she said. But she saw the shallow flight of stone steps Meggie had told them to look for, leading down to a shadowy doorway. "Come on! We'll be late. Maybe Eliza is already waiting." Eliza had said she would meet them there after her shift at the factory, though they hadn't seen her for a while.

She tugged Charlotte down the steps after her and knocked three times on the door. A tiny, grilled window set high above her head slid open.

"The elephant's eyebrows," she said, repeating the passwords she'd been given. Obviously, someone there had a weird sense of humor.

The window slammed shut, and for several long seconds there was no sound except that distant hum of cars and the pounding of Jessica's heart. Had she done it wrong? Had she come this close to finding a real story, to finding her shipboard Romeo again, only to be turned away?

Finally, the door swung open. A huge Gorgon of a man stood before them, so large he seemed about to burst the seams of his fine dinner jacket. His eyes, deep-set under the bushy brows of his bald head, stared down at them.

Charlotte clutched at Jessica's hand, and even Jess had a flash of unease.

"Come in, then," the giant said in a deep, guttural accent she couldn't quite place. "Can't keep the door open all night, the cats get in."

Nothing to do but jump, then. Jessica pulled Charlotte in behind her, the door slid shut, closing out the night. He led them down another steep staircase.

"What's your name?" Jessica asked him.

"It's Tiny," he growled, holding out a hand to help her down a dimly lit step. Jessica couldn't help but giggle. "What's the big deal, then?"

"Nothing at all, er, Tiny," she answered. "I'm sure it suits you."

"Huh," he growled again, but she had the sense he was about to laugh, just before he lumbered away to answer another knock.

A woman in a black and white maid's uniform

stepped forward silently to take their coats. Jessica barely had time to smooth down the skirt of her dark blue, lavender-beaded dress and straighten her feathered headband before another door opened, and Club 501 itself was revealed.

"Oh," she gasped before she could stop herself. Charlotte's gloved hand tightened on hers.

Jessica had seen some beautiful places in her life. Buckingham Palace, where she curtsied to the queen on her debut; the Ritz Hotel ballroom, where Lord Leicester trod on her new satin shoes during their waltz; country houses hundreds of years old. But nothing quite so enticing as this.

Being hidden deep under the street, the club was large enough to rise to two levels, but small enough to feel luxuriously intimate. A mezzanine looked down on the crowded dance floor, lined with round tables and with velvet banquettes tucked into darkened corners. Along one side of the floor ran a long, polished oak bar, backed by glass shelves lit from beneath to showcase an array of the precious, illegal bottles. All good stuff with real labels, pale gold or deep amber; no bathtub hooch there.

At the far end of the oblong room was a stage. A jazz band, drums, horns, a piano, flashed in the background just beyond the footlights, and Meggie stood in front of them, softly spotlit in her new gold satin dress with metallic fringe that caught and reflected every spark of light. She leaned close to the microphone, her eyes closed as she crooned a soft ballad to the couples who moved slowly around the light-ringed floor.

"Can I help you, ladies?" someone said behind

them in a light, silvery voice.

Jessica spun around and almost gasped again. It was the countess who stood there, the exotically gorgeous woman from the ship! She was just as pale and Snow Queen-ish as before, if not more so. She wore black silk, unadorned but perfectly cut to flow sensuously around her slender figure. Pearls were wound around her throat and formed a headband around her brow.

She gave a knowing smile, almost a little smirk that made Jessica feel like a gawky schoolgirl again. She drew herself up and gave the woman the same expression Queen Mary had once given all the hapless debs. "We were invited here tonight."

"I am Countess Markova, hostess here at Club 501," the woman said, her smile fading a bit. "May I find you a seat on the mezzanine? Perhaps send for some champagne?"

"Thank you, that would be lovely," Jessica answered haughtily.

"Are you sure we should stay?" Charlotte whispered.

"Of course," Jess whispered back. "We have as much right to be here as anyone."

The countess led them up a winding staircase to a small table right next to the railing looking down on the dance floor. Charlotte twisted her head around this way and that, peering as closely as she could without her specs at everything around them.

Jessica was tempted to do just the same, but she made herself remember her mother's old lectures on being dignified and kept her head high and a cool smile on her lips. She didn't want the ridiculously chic countess thinking she had anything over Lord Hatton's daughter!

Nor did she want anyone getting suspicious before she even had the chance of finding a good story. As far as the countess, or anyone else, had to know, Jess was just there to drink and dance, like everyone else.

If Charlotte's gawking didn't ruin things first. Jessica pulled on her hand to make her move forward up the last steps to the table where the countess waited.

"Did you see that woman over there in the red dress?" Charlotte whispered. "That was Maude Andrews, the film star! I was just reading about her in *Cinema Talk*. They say she's getting a divorce from her husband so she can marry a French marquis. Do you suppose that's him with her now?"

Jessica carefully peeked at Miss Andrews and her dark-mustached, pomade-haired escort. They didn't look at each other or at anyone else, but there was the definite sense of posing about them, as if they expected everyone around them to notice their perfect profiles. Jessica was sure if that was the sort of people who came to Club 501, she could always find juicy tidbits for the society pages if a real story didn't present itself. But hopefully it wouldn't come to that.

The countess held out the gilded chairs and gave them another cool smile. "Shall I send up some champagne, mesdames? We have a very fine vintage, just arrived."

Jessica glanced over the railing at the dance floor and the bar below. Surely there would be plenty of gentlemen there who would want to buy them drinks.

"That would be lovely, thank you," Jessica said with an equally cool smile.

The countess glided away, stopping to speak to a waiter, who soon arrived at their table with glasses of golden, effervescent champagne. Charlotte was quickly claimed for a foxtrot, but Jessica waved away hopeful partners for the time being. It was hard to keep an eye on things while whirling around on the dance floor.

"Just go have fun!" she called to Charlotte as her friend gave her an agonized glance over the new partner's shoulder. "It's good for you."

She sipped at her wine, which was indeed a "very fine vintage," much better than the syrupy concoctions to be found at other bars they had visited in New York. As she let its delicious warmth flood through her, she tapped her toe and studied the room closer. It was more crowded now than when they first arrived, with more couples in well-cut dark suits and satin gowns flowing around in the dance, more people clustered around the bar, as Meggie sang out louder and louder.

At last, as Meggie's voice soared up to a wild crescendo, Jessica caught a glimpse of what she sought. Her dark swain from the ship.

He stood at the bar talking to a very tall bartender, laughing. He did look gorgeous when he laughed, his eyes lighter, his face more relaxed, like some rakish pirate from a novel banned at Mrs. Greensley's. He was as well-dressed as any of the rich customers, in a beautifully tailored French evening suit, his dark hair glossy in the faint light.

He half-turned as the countess came up to him and touched his arm. He bent his head to listen as she whispered in his ear, and though he kept smiling, Jessica thought she saw a dark shadow drift over his absurdly handsome face. He studied the room with narrowed eyes.

He spoke briefly to the bartender again and then stalked off through a hidden door in the dark-paneled wall behind the bar. No one seemed to notice what he did.

Jessica knew she had to find out what was in there. She almost laughed aloud with a sudden giddy feeling of fear and raw excitement, all mixed up inside of her.

She gulped down the last of her champagne and pushed herself up from the table before she could think about it all too much. If she was going to get all cautious now, she thought, she might as well have stayed in England!

The carpeted floor beneath her velvet shoes vibrated with the force of the music and the swirl of the dancers. Meggie was singing *Chime's Blues* now, her arms raised and bangle bracelets flashing as she moved to the tune. The floor was even more crowded now, like a fragmented stained-glass window of bright colors.

Along with the music, the booze was also flowing. Jessica had to fend off several offers to dance as she made her way down the stairs and around the main floor. A few of them were a bit insistent, and she had to discourage one with a sharp heel to his instep. She pushed him away, and he was caught by his friends, who laughed at him uproariously as he bellowed after her. She just ignored him and kept moving; she had bigger fish to fry, for sure.

The crowd's wild gaiety gave her the perfect cover. She crept around the edge of the bar. The bartender, a young, distinctively tall and handsome man in a red waistcoat, was very busy. People were clamoring for drinks faster than he could mix them. There was no sign of the countess or of Jessica's matinee idol from the ship.

Unnoticed, she managed to push through the hidden door. She slid it closed behind her and found herself facing a long, narrow, dark corridor.

For a minute, she could barely see or hear anything after the abrupt change from the whirl of light and noise from the club. The heavy wooden door against her back vibrated with the muffled music and laughter.

She blinked hard and saw that she wasn't really in complete darkness. There was another door at the end of the corridor, mostly closed, but open a tiny crack that let out a ray of light. There was only a very narrow walkway between towering stacks of crates. They were all stamped "Orange Juice—Product of Florida."

Jessica took a deep breath to steady herself and smelled mingled dust and booze. She took a step forward and nearly fell down a shallow set of wooden stairs. The hall went down and then forward, twisting away from the reassuring light and noise of the party.

She tiptoed between the crates, keeping her eye firmly on that door. Above her head, there was a muffled roar, as if she was passing under the street, and she shivered.

After what seemed like hours but could only have been a couple of minutes, she finally got close to the door. Beyond it, the corridor veered sharply away, leading even farther into the depths below the city. She heard the low, rough murmur of voices, smelled a whiff of cigar smoke. At last, she was so, so close...

Then she realized—those voices were speaking Russian.

Drat it all! She cursed silently, ruing the fact that

her governess and Mrs. Greensley's only taught "ladylike" French. Surely something fascinatingly illegal was going on in there, and she had no way of finding out what it was just by eavesdropping.

She ducked quickly behind a stack of more crates and dug out her little notebook and pencil from her handbag. Maybe she could write down how some of the words sounded and figure it out later. She scribbled down some of the words, and suddenly there was a laugh, as low and rich and dark as a fine whiskey. Surely that was *his* laugh.

Suddenly, the door was pulled open hard, knocking loudly into some crates. Jessica almost jumped, cursing herself for being so inattentive. She shrank down even farther, crouching on the gritty floor as she peeked out between the slats of her hiding place.

A tall, burly man stumbled out of the room. Unlike the men in the bar, he was roughly dressed in a brown wool jacket and checked cap, young, handsome but hard-faced. He strode across the corridor, and Jessica heard the unmistakable sound of a trouser zip just before he actually started to urinate. She pressed her hand hard to her mouth, afraid she might burst into hysterical laughter.

But the good part of a man suddenly needing the loo was that he left the door ajar. Careful not to let any of the light fall on her, she peered inside.

She saw the man from the ship, the owner of Club 501, sitting at a table with a few other men, all of them dressed like the man in the hall. A bottle of clear vodka and a few glasses were scattered around amid stacks of papers. Their faces all looked most solemn as they talked together in low voices.

"Yevgeny!" someone shouted, followed by a string of words she couldn't make out.

"Butch the bookkeeper here has something to say about the numbers," someone else said.

"*Da, da*," the urinator called back. He mercifully zipped back up before he went back into the room and closed the door. Darkness closed around her.

Jessica sighed. It seemed she would get no more secret peeps tonight. She tucked her notebook, with its sloppy phonetic Russian words, back in her beaded bag and carefully made her way back down the dim corridor of "orange juice."

She managed to slip back into the party just as unnoticed as she left. Relief and excitement flooded over her, and she pushed her way through the crowd around the bar to get a bright pink drink from the tall bartender. She looked around, still trembling with her own daring, and saw that Charlotte was still dancing, her eyes wide and startled. She hadn't been able to escape yet. Meggie was taking a break, sharing a smoke with the trumpet player.

She went up on tiptoe to survey the crowd again. She glimpsed Eliza across the room, talking to a man in an expensive but ill-fitting brown suit, his belly hanging over his belt. Eliza smiled, but something about her expression looked uncertain. Jessica took a step toward her, only to be abruptly pulled back.

"You're a pretty little duckie, now, ain't you?" a rough, slurred voice said at her elbow. Whoever it belonged to jostled into her, almost making her spill her precious new drink. A hard hand pinched at her backside, and she jumped.

She spun around and glared at the man who leaned

on the bar next to her. He was sweaty and clammy, leering down at her with reddened eyes. He smelled heavily of the cheapest gin. Nothing she hadn't faced down before.

"I beg your pardon?" she said, in imitation of her mother's frostiest Lady Hatton voice.

"Ooh, a posh duckie," he slurred. "Come and dance with me, love. I can show you a grand time."

Jessica raked a scathing glance over his sweat-stained suit and clammy hands. "No, thank you," she said, turning away.

He grabbed her arm roughly. "Hey, girlie, you should be more friendly," he growled, more menacing than she had given him credit for. "All the ladies like Joey Keegan."

"Not this lady!" She tried to yank away from him, feeling suddenly nervous.

"The lady declined to dance," someone said, in a low, dark Russian accent. That someone stepped between her and the grabber. A tall, lean someone in a perfectly cut black evening suit. A someone who smelled of a light, spicy cologne and ever so faintly of cigar smoke. His handsome, austerely carved face seemed made of stone.

"There's a lot more friendly places around here, y'know, where I could spend my money," the grabber blustered.

"I suggest you go patronize one of those places, then," her rescuer said calmly. "We are not that sort of establishment at Club 501. Ladies are free to dance here with no fear of being accosted."

"Accosted!" the man shouted. "I did no such thing. I'll have you know who I am..."

"Tiny, please see the gentleman to the street," her rescuer said, summoning the burly doorkeeper with a flick of his hand.

The drunken lout was unceremoniously carried out, the crowd gathering in behind him and drowning out his incoherent shouts. The Russian turned to Jessica with a smile. She noticed that he still had that horribly distracting dimple right in his cheek, tempting her to reach out and touch it. Drat the man.

"So," he said, still smiling. "We meet again."

Jessica gathered her composure around her again and smiled back. If she could just keep smiling—it was one of the valuable lessons she had learned from the hard task of being a deb. "So we do," she said. She was afraid she was staring up at him like a Dumb Dora, not a sophisticated city lady who often frequented high-class speakeasies, but she just couldn't help it. He was way too handsome. Way too much like a puzzle she couldn't quite figure out.

And her curiosity over puzzles had always gotten the better of her.

But she reminded herself she had to be careful now. After all, he was a handsome guy who hung around with Russian bruisers in back rooms.

"Thanks for the save," she said. She took a cigarette from her handbag and let him light it for her. She noticed the lighter was made of silver, engraved with a Cyrillic monogram set with diamonds and turquoise. Was it Faberge? His hand was sun-browned and strong, not like he spent all of his time buried under the street in a dark bar, and a long, thin white scar cut across the back of it.

"Such behavior has no place here," he said. "I

don't think we had time for proper introductions on the *Empress of India*, did we, mademoiselle? I'm Frank Markov."

Jessica kept smiling up at him through the silvery wreath of smoke. Frank Markov, huh? Maybe the Markov part, she thought. But Frank? Really? Maybe Nicolai, or Dimitri.

He did look Russian, though. She thought of the aristocratic families who had taken refuge at estates near Hatton Hall, their lean, finely-drawn faces, their high cheekbones and musical accents, their fine manners, the courtly French they had used so much at home in Russia. He would fit in with them perfectly.

"You own this place, right?" she said.

His dark, raven's-wing brow arched. "So I do. But I hope not everyone knows that."

Jessica laughed. "Don't worry, I don't read minds. My roommate is your new singer." She nodded toward the stage, where Meggie was singing again.

"Ah, so that is where I saw her last," he said with an amused smile. "She was with you on the ship. I have thought much of our dance since then, mademoiselle."

She was startled by his words. She'd been completely sure he forgot about her the moment they parted on the dance floor. "I don't see how you could have had time for much thinking at all, getting this place set up and all. It's swell."

"But you are most memorable, mademoiselle, as I'm sure you know," he answered. His smile faded, and his icy blue eyes narrowed as he studied her. "I'm glad to find you again in this vast city, and looking so well. Even if you haven't yet told me your name."

"It's Jessica. Jess."

"English Jessica. What brings you to New York?"

She shrugged. "What brings anyone here? Work, love, a bit of excitement. England has been a bit drab since the war. I wanted a change of scene."

Drab, yes, but nothing compared to the devastation of *his* country, she feared. Those handsome Russians she met after they fled St. Petersburg were all filled with sadness and hard smiles and few words about their homeland. But there were always lurid stories in the papers her parents thought she didn't read. She studied his gorgeous face and longed to ask him what had brought him here.

"We can't have drab, now can we?" he said with a laugh. "Will you dance with me again, Jessica? I think I could be a bit more polished than your admirer Mr. Keegan. I won't have to be chucked out."

Jessica was deeply tempted. She remembered all too well how it felt when he took her in his arms for a dance. How she felt so excited, but oddly so safe, all at the same time.

But she glanced past his shoulder to see Charlotte waving at her through the crowd. She looked rather eager to leave, as it was growing more packed by the minute, louder, hotter. Eliza and the man in the brown suit were nowhere to be seen.

"Not tonight, I'm afraid," she said regretfully. Some sort of criminal he might be, but surely one more dance couldn't have hurt anything? "Not a commentary on your dance skills at all, Mr. Markov. My friend over there tells me it's time to go. Our coach is about to turn into a pumpkin."

He brow crinkled in a puzzled frown that was terribly adorable. "Pumpkin? Is a vegetable, no?"

Jessica laughed. "It's from an old story my nanny used to tell me—Cinderella. You don't know it?"

He shook his head. "My nanny used to tell me of Baba Yaga."

"Baba Yaga? I never heard of that one. The name sounds frightful."

"And so she was, a terrible witch who lived in the woods in a cottage made of bones. I will tell it to you one day, if you will tell me of your Cinderella."

How she wished she *could* tell him. She could sit beside him listening to his deep, rich voice all day if he'd let her, hoping to make him laugh again. Even as she knew she really shouldn't, she said, "It's a deal."

"Then I will see you again at Club 501?"

Jessica nodded and turned away from the noisy bar. She walked away while she still could. She quickly found Charlotte again, and they made their way to the stairs leading up to the street outside. To the real world.

Only at the door did she dare take one teeny glance back. Frank Markov was watching her, too, a frown on his face. He saw her watching and smiled, giving her a wave, but she could still see that shadow in his eyes.

"Oh, Jess, you will never guess what happened!" Charli said as they took their coats from the maid and ducked back out into the warm, silent night.

"You met a handsome prince?" Jessica said whimsically, her thoughts still half with Mr. Markov.

Charli made a scoffing sound. "Better. I obtained a position at Club 501!"

"You did?" Jessica answered in surprise. That was by far the boldest thing Charlotte had done since coming to New York. "Singing like Meggie?"

"Of course not. You know I sound like a dying frog

when I try to sing. It's much better! They need a waitress, which doesn't sound very interesting, I know. But I heard some famous French chef sometimes comes here, maybe I can meet him and ask him for some cooking tips later."

Charlotte went on talking about the new job, and Jessica could only think about how useful it would be to have *two* friends working there. Two friends who could get the dirt on Mr. Frank Markov.

Only now she kind of hoped there was really no dirt on him at all...

Chapter Six

Red Menace Tide Drowns New York!

Jessica took a sip of tea and tried not to snort it back out as she read the blocky, screaming black letters of the headline. Thank goodness that wasn't the paper *she* worked for, she thought. Writing about hats and rosebushes was bad enough, but at least she didn't have to write articles that incited people to ignorant panic. Red tide indeed.

On the other hand...

She remembered the men in that back room at Club 501, their Russian accents and rough clothes. Surely they were just a bunch of bootleggers negotiating over new shipments, but they *were* Russian.

As was Mr. Markov. *Frank Markov.* Jessica sighed as she thought about him yet again. She hadn't been able to sleep at all after she stumbled into bed in the wee, wee hours. She'd lain awake on her narrow bed, seeing his handsome face in her mind, going over every word he said to her, every inflection of his whiskey-smooth voice.

She was no closer to understanding him at all. In fact, she was even more confused.

He didn't look like the sort to consort with Yevgeny types. Too well-dressed, too elegant, too educated with his perfect English. Then again, he did run a speakeasy, not exactly a respectable trade. Even one as swanky as Club 501.

She took another sip of tea and frowned down at the newspaper again. She wondered what Frank Markov had done before New York. In Russia. Perhaps he had been an officer in the war or fought for the White Russians as the "red menace" overran his country. Maybe that was where he got those scars. Or maybe he'd been one of those aristos who joined up with the Bolshies in a flood of idealism, only to be betrayed and run out. She'd heard stories about people like that. One princess she met in a London ballroom said her own daughter-in-law had denounced the family and taken up arms for the reds.

The dramatic possibilities for a man like Markov were endless.

Jessica sighed and pushed away the paper, reaching for one of Charlotte's scones to nibble on. She liked the early mornings in the flat when everyone else was asleep and she had a quiet hour to finish her tea and think without the endless clacking typewriters at the paper. It was exciting at the office, with so much stuff always going on, but impossible to plan.

And she needed a plan now.

She glanced at the curtain that closed off the bedroom door. Eliza had never come home at all, and Meggie had fallen into bed at dawn, her dancing shoes still strapped on, and immediately gone asleep. Surely Meggie would be able to tell her more about what it was like at Club 501 once she had her own tea and some time to be coherent again. But that would take a while.

Jessica drew her kimono closer around her and reached for one of the more respectable newspapers scattered across the rickety old kitchen table. It, too, had a story on the Bolsheviks infiltrating New York, but not worded in such a lurid way. It speculated on what the new president, to be elected in only a few weeks, might do about the Red threat. About where it was lurking now.

Jessica frowned. Was *that* what was happening at Club 501? Secret anarchist meetings? She thought again of the stories the Russian refugees at home told of their lost homes and families, and she shivered.

A vision of Frank Markov's blue eyes flashed through her mind, and she realized she was dumb enough to not *want* to believe it of him.

She had to find out what was really happening at Club 501.

****

The typewriters were clacking at full speed when Jessica stepped through the doors of the *World*. Secretaries and young cub reporters ran past her, their arms full of notebooks and files. It was close to the deadline hour, and the hot smell of ink and cheap paper was thick in the air.

Jessica hurried to her own desk and hung up her hat and coat. The information about Mrs. Astor's garden club was still piled on her desk, but she ignored it for now. Instead she turned on her heel and went to the archives room where back issues were stored.

Luckily, Mrs. Mortimer, the draconian librarian, wasn't on duty. Paul, the young man with a crush on her, was manning the front desk with the catalogs. Jessica felt terrible about using his crush against him, but sometimes needs must.

"Hiya, Paul," she said, leaning against the counter.

"Mrs. Mortimer out today?"

"At the printer for a few," Paul answered with a grin. "How can I help you, Jess?"

"I need any information you have on the anarchist story," she said, trying to seem casual, as if it was just a passing, gossipy interest. "My parents knew some White Russians in London, they were always warning about stuff like that, but they never said what a revolutionary might look like."

But Walter was easygoing, not dumb. His grin turned sharp. "This for your new Mrs. Astor story, then? Doesn't sound like it."

"Not really. Just curiosity, I suppose."

"Well, if I show it to you, let me know if you find anything interesting."

"Of course," Jessica said with a smile, hoping he wouldn't ask her out again as the price for helping her in the archives.

He brought her boxes full of clippings, which she sorted through as quickly as she could. The stories looked fascinating, but she had her garden party story to get started with and couldn't be distracted. Finally, near the bottom of the pile, she found something really interesting.

Mrs. Schuyler's Daughter Nursing in Europe! read a headline from 1915. There was a fading, grainy photo of a pretty girl in a white-veiled uniform standing behind a mustachioed soldier in a wheelchair, two others standing to either side of her. She smiled, but the men looked solemn, guarded. One of them was a younger Frank Markov.

Startled, Jessica quickly scanned the story. Miss Schuyler, it seemed had spent time training at the Grand

Duchess Tatiana's hospital near St. Petersburg, but the reporter seemed more concerned with the titled royalty she had met than with her work. The man was identified as "Prince Nicolai," but Jessica was sure it was Frank. His dark hair was slightly shorter, but the austerely sculpted features were the same, the wary smile, the tall, lean figure in his uniform. So he *was* some sort of Russian royalty. Why would he be consorting with Bolshies now?

She quickly tucked the article into her pocket and tidied the other folders into a neat pile. "Thanks, Walter," she called over her shoulder as she hurried out of the room. "You're a peach..."

She had to get back to Club 501 and find some answers.

Chapter Seven

"Back again, are you, miss?" the tall bartender said with a grin as Jessica pushed her way between the massed crowds at the bar. Club 501 had obviously lost none of its popularity in the two nights since she had been there. "We must be doing something right."

Jessica laughed and gestured to the room around her, the scads of glittering dancers, the jostling packs clamoring for a drink. "I'd say you are. Surely no place in the city could be more popular."

"That's because of all the pretty girls that come here."

"I know! You have two of my friends working here now." She nodded toward Meggie, singing in the spotlight in a purple beaded gown, and Charlotte making her way between the tables in a smart new wine-red silk dress, a tray of drinks balancing in her hands.

"We'll have you working here next. I need an apprentice bartender," he teased.

Jessica laughed. "Tempting, but I'm afraid I already have a job." If you could call it that, with all those endless descriptions of flower arrangements and lace trim on gowns, and Mrs. Mortimer chasing her out of the archives. "So, what's your name, bartender?"

"Ira," he answered. "Pleased to meet you, miss."

"Pleased to meet you." She glanced at the hidden

door behind the bar, barely visible now in the dark paneling and the faint lighting. Maybe her garden party days would be behind her soon.

But would it be at the expense of Mr. Markov?

"What'll you have, then, miss?" the bartender asked. "I have a new creation of my own, a pomegranate infused gin with champagne. Matches your dress."

Jessica laughed and smoothed down the skirt of her gold-embroidered dark red gown. "I'll try that, then, thanks." She took her fresh drink, which was indeed a lovely, sparkly red color, and made her way slowly around the dance floor. It was even more crowded tonight than before, the dancers swirling closer to the bar. There were also more mysterious, hard-faced men in black suits, and she couldn't quite figure out how to get into the hidden tunnel unseen. Tiny was watching too closely from the front doors.

Suddenly, she caught a glimpse of her quarry. Frank Markov, spotlit by one of the fringed silk-covered lamps, his dark hair shining, his pale eyes watchful. She couldn't quite breathe for a second.

He was chatting with a couple at a table just at the edge of the dance floor, smiling at something the diamond-bedecked lady was saying. He wore his perfectly-cut evening suit again and a soft black tie that made him look austere and perfectly expensive. Just like in that old photo, he had not lost his officer's proud bearing.

She thought of the article in that silly paper again. *The Red Menace!* Markov didn't look much like a Bolshevik. According to her mother, they were all burly hooligans with unkempt beards. If anything, he looked like the aristocratic officers her sister Lulu danced with during the war while Jessica sneaked out of the nursery to peek down at the ballroom in the middle of the night. They came from everywhere in Europe, France, Italy, Russia, all tall and handsome, dashing and so often sadly doomed.

But Markov ran a speakeasy. No matter ridiculous the America law, or how everyone flouted it, that *would* technically make him a criminal. And there were those Russians in the secret room...

Jessica frowned as she remembered that scene. She knew very well how dangerous it could all be; look what happened to the people who opposed them in Russia. Yet she had to know what was really going on here.

She straightened the skirt of her red dancing dress and pushed the short strands of her red hair behind her ears. She would never be equal in looks to Markov's dark matinee idol face, but at least she looked presentable in her best dress. She blended in well enough.

She made her way toward Markov, sipping at her drink, keeping her eye on him as he chatted with the customers.

Finally, they met at the corner of the dance floor.

"So we meet again, mademoiselle," he said with a smile. He didn't seem at all surprised to see her there.

"I can't seem to stay away from the music," she answered brightly. "You've certainly created a swell joint here, Mr. Markov."

"We shouldn't let the lovely song go to waste, then," he said. "Will you dance with me this time?"

Jessica was afraid she couldn't quite breathe when

he smiled like that. She knew she *had* to dance with him. She could only nod. He took her half-finished drink from her hand and gave it to a passing waitress before he took Jessica in his arms. He moved into the flow of dancers as smoothly as a fine silk scarf, drawing her with him into the swirling waltz. He felt so hard and warm under her hand, his smell so clean and crisp it wound around her like a spell.

The crowd around them pressed her much closer to him than would ever be proper in Mayfair. She held onto him tightly to keep from being lost, one hand on his shoulder, the other clasped in his cool, strong hand. His long fingers felt callused, as if he didn't just chat and drink for his job, and a ring she couldn't see on his smallest finger pressed lightly into her skin.

The grace and lightness she remembered from their dance on the ship came out, guiding her steps as they wove through the other dancers. One—two—three, one—two—three, just like every waltz but completely different. Jessica couldn't help herself. She rested her head against his chest and closed her eyes. The song was slow and languid, all the couples around them swaying close to each other, wrapped up in the romantic music, the low light, the smell of expensive perfume and wine and smoke.

Jessica let herself let go of everything for a moment—her family, her job, her suspicions and fears—and let the music just wrap around her, too. The warmth of Frank Markov's strong, hard body seeped through her, into her. Despite everything, she found she had never felt quite so *safe* in her life.

Safe. With a man whose real name she suspected she didn't even know.

Their steps slid together perfectly, her sequined T-strap shoes between his polished patent evening pumps, their bodies fitting as if they had always been just like that. She thought of all the dances at those deb parties, how awkward they were, how never-ending. Not at all like this one.

She thought she would happily go on dancing like that all night long, winding around the floor with Frank Markov until they could fly up spiraling into the stars. But of course the song ended all too soon, and Jessica had to shake away those shimmering clouds of dreams. She tilted back her head and looked up at him. He smiled down at her, but she couldn't read the expression in his icy blue eyes.

"Would you sit with me for a moment, mademoiselle? Have a drink?" he said.

"Of course," Jessica murmured.

She followed him to a quiet table tucked beside the bar near the stage and let him hold out the chair for her. She studied him as he gestured for two glasses of champagne. He looked so at ease, so elegant. What was his game here?

"I confess I find you most intriguing, mademoiselle," he said with a crooked, entirely too charming smile.

"Me?" Jessica said with a laugh. Her laugh, easy and careless, always put off the boys at home, distracted them, made them look only at her carefully constructed facade. "I am completely ordinary."

But it seemed in this, like everything else, Frank Markov was nothing like those boys. He looked at her steadily, solemnly, as if he wasn't fooled by her light laughter at all. "I think you are the furthest thing from ordinary."

Jessica shrugged and took a drink of the champagne. She felt suddenly giddy, fuzzy-headed. What could be in that drink? She was afraid it was only him that had such an effect on her, not the alcohol at all. "I work every day, I like a drink and a dance in the evening, like every modern girl."

Markov laughed, and it brought out that adorable dimple, making him look eons younger and lighter. "You are certainly most *modern*. But I think I have never met a girl quite like you. What has brought you all the way to New York? I think your family in England must miss you."

Jessica shook her head. She didn't want to think about Lulu, and Mummy and Dad, how they must be so disappointed in her. "They're much too busy to miss me, I bet."

"And you will go back there soon?"

That was what Jessica feared. She would fail in her ambitions here, ambitions her family thought were silly, and have to go home to marry one of those Eton boys. Yes, eventually she *would* have to face them. She just wanted it to be on her terms. "Maybe. I'm having too much fun in New York right now."

"Is it usual in fine English families to send their daughters across the ocean alone?"

"How do you know my family is so very fine?" Jessica said as she tried to laugh.

Markov laughed, too, but she sensed he wasn't fooled. "Your accent, for one. Your looks. That gown. Patou, yes?"

How did he know where her dress came from? Drat the man. "We all have a right to remake ourselves, don't we? Look at you, Mr. Markov."

"Me?" he said, his smile fading.

"You're surely no peasant, either, I'm sure. There are many Russian refugees who live near my parents. Countesses and princes. I think it would be hard to imitate their manners—or hide them."

"You are quite right," he said with an unreadable little smile. He turned his glass between his fingers, and she saw the champagne was hardly touched. A silver ring on his finger flashed, but she couldn't study it in the faint light. "This is a wondrous new world we live in. Anything can happen to anyone."

Jessica studied his handsome face. With the smile gone, he looked older, harder. Haunted, even. Surely whatever he hid was far more dangerous than her own little secrets. But in that instant the noise and the crowd faded around them, and she could only see him. He looked into her eyes, and she saw flash of raw pain there. Then it was hidden in another smile.

She knew then that, no matter what they each hid in their own hearts, he really saw her, as no one else ever had. They were two of a kind. Risk takers. Curious. Wild.

It was exciting, new, wondrous—and it made her want to run away even as she never wanted to leave.

"Shall we dance again?" he said quietly.

"I—I'm afraid I must be going," she stammered. "It's very late, and I'm sure you have a lot of work to do. You shouldn't waste any more of your evening talking to me."

"But talking to you is the most fascinating thing I've done in a very long time," he said. She would have thought he would be joking, teasing, but there was none of that in his low, rough tone.

"Thank you for the champagne." Jessica quickly slid out of her chair and ducked into the crowd before he could follow. She couldn't think straight when he looked at her.

Just before she turned to leave the bar area, she surreptitiously pushed at the hidden door in the paneling. It was firmly locked. She didn't know if she was disappointed—or relieved.

At the top of the stairs, she glanced back, but Frank Markov was nowhere to be seen.

Chapter Eight

"And here we have the famous Malmaison rose, which was especially bred in France for this very spot in the greenhouses," Mrs. Astor said as she led a crowd of avidly listening ladies along the winding pathways of the vast glass greenhouse behind her grand graytone townhouse, made to look like a French chateau.

All Jessica could see was a sea of hats, all pale straw and pastel silks, bedecked with satin flowers, glistening wax fruit, and fluttering chiffon ribbons. She glanced down at her notebook about Elizabethan herb beds and Italian climbing clematis, as well as descriptions of what all the society ladies of the garden club were wearing. She was sure it was more than enough information to make a properly fawning article, one the socially-gossipy *World* readership would eat up and Mrs. Astor would appreciate for getting her name out there yet again for all her good works.

Surely Jessica had earned a little break.

She glanced toward the terrace, where tea and lemonade were laid out amid elaborate flower arrangements in Wedgewood vases. Mr. Astor stood there in his fine white suit, in a group of other bored-looking gentlemen who had been talking endlessly about the upcoming presidential election. Jessica recognized the chief of police, a couple of judges, and the owner of a large railroad company, among others.

They didn't look like their crystal glasses held lemonade.

She left the garden group, all of them now listening wide-eyed as Mrs. Astor talked about the new orangery under construction behind her house, and made her way to one of the white tents laid out by the terrace. The pink-draped tables were still covered with more silver teapots and china platters laden with half-eaten petit fours and cucumber sandwiches. The pink and yellow roses in their silver urns were drooping.

Jessica was afraid she was drooping, too. She brushed off her limp green silk dress and took off her green velvet cloche hat to shake her hair free. She made her way to one of the waiters who was desultorily clearing away the plates.

"There wouldn't happen to be something a wee bit stronger than tea over here, would there?" she asked hopefully, thinking of the amber liquor Mr. Astor and his guests on the terrace were sipping.

He laughed, his bored face brightening a bit. "There just might be, miss. A special tea, you might say."

He gave her a teacup filled with smoky, lovely amber brandy slightly tinted with tea. She took it with her and wandered back out to the garden, below the men hiding on the terrace.

"Miss Hatton, what a pleasure to see you here," she heard a deep, smooth, Russian voice say behind her, and she spun around in startled excitement.

It *was* Frank Markov. In the very last place she ever would have expected to find him. Yet he seemed to belong there in that elegant garden, in a fine suit and gray fedora, a faint smile on his sensual lips.

"And you, Mr. Markov," she answered. And it was true. It *was* very good to see him, and the dull day suddenly seemed a hundred times more intriguing. "I wouldn't have thought a garden party was quite your scene."

"I have many new friends here in New York," he said. He glanced back at the terrace, and Jessica followed his gaze to the men gathered there. Mr. Astor was passing around the cigars to senators and railway heirs, which was no doubt where Frank had been, yet he chose to come down into the garden with her. Interesting indeed.

Frank still smiled, but she had the strange sense that something had changed in it as two of the men waved at him. "Would you care to walk with me for a few minutes, Miss Hatton? Mrs. Astor's flowers are quite lovely."

"Of course," she said, even more intrigued than ever. She took his offered arm, feeling the tense, muscled strength of it under her fingers. He smelled delicious, like something lemony and clean and enticing. He led her down one of the rose-lined paths, away from the chattering crowds.

They soon found themselves on a walkway around an ornamental Oriental pond, heavy with dark green shade, koi fish like flickers of gold in the depths of the mossy water. It was cool and serene, like a whole different world.

"How are you enjoying the New York parties?" he said with a laugh. "Different from London, yes?"

Jessica laughed with him. "Not so very different, no. But really I'm just working today."

"Working?"

She held up her little notebook. "I write for the *New York World*. Did you not know?"

He frowned, his expression hidden by the brim of his hat. "You are a reporter?"

"Yes. Well, no, not really. I write little things like descriptions of parties and charity events. Hats and gowns." How silly it sounded when she said it like that. She suddenly wanted so very much to be anything but silly in front of him.

He didn't laugh at her, though. "Ah. I had a cousin who did such things in Russia. Our family quite disapproved."

"Your cousin wrote for a newspaper?" Jessica asked, puzzled.

"For a court newspaper, about how the dowager empress was opening a school or a princess had a debut ball."

Jessica was rather intrigued by this tiny glimpse of his past, his family. "That's sort of what I do. But I bet it was much more exciting in St. Petersburg."

"It was a different world then," he said simply, and there seemed a world of emotion behind those simple words. But he said no more.

They had come to a small summerhouse set on the banks of the pond, a fantasy of enameled red and black with latticed walls and curved rooflines. "This looks rather like something at my parents' home," she said, suddenly feeling a pang of homesickness. "My sister and I used to have tea parties there when we were children, and our brother would secretly swim up and splash on our careful arrangements."

Frank laughed. "Rather like families everywhere, I imagine. What do your siblings do now? Do they also write?"

"Lulu is a newlywed. And Bill..." Jessica saw her brother's face in her mind, so laughing and open, so full of fun. She turned her face away in a sudden flood of sadness. "Bill died in the war."

"I am so very sorry. Too many fine men were lost."

Jessica glanced up at him, batting away the tears that threatened to fall. Frank looked sad, too, so solemn and understanding. His dignified sympathy made her want to run and hide but also to throw herself into his strong arms and hide from the pain of the past, the uncertainty of the future. Impulsively, she grabbed his hand and pulled him behind her up the steps into the black and red shadows of the summerhouse.

There, in the waving, dream-like pattern of sunlight, he looked so sad. Lost—just as she had felt for so very long. Here was surely a man who could understand her at last. She was overcome with the crazy urge to kiss him.

Jessica stepped closer to him, as if drawn in by some power she couldn't see but was completely helpless to resist. He stood very still, as taut and wary as some jungle cat holding back its strength, watching her with narrowed eyes that no longer looked like ice.

She wrapped her hands around the lapels of his fine wool jacket and went up on tiptoe. Gently, softly, still not completely sure what she was doing, she kissed the very corner of his mouth. Then she kissed the other, feeling the leashed strength of him under her hands.

He gave a deep growl, low in his throat, and suddenly his arms came around her, pulling her close, and his lips claimed hers as he took control of the kiss.

Jessica's mouth parted on a startled gasp, and she

felt the touch of his tongue on hers, tasting her, exploring her. When those boys back in London had tried that, it seemed somehow vile and filled her with impatience. But here, with this one infuriatingly attractive man, it felt wonderfully delightful. A delicious, giddy heat seemed to build up deep inside of her. What did that mean? She certainly didn't want to stop and consider it all. She just wanted to feel more of that wonderfulness.

She twined her arms around his neck and went up on her toes, letting him deepen the kiss even more. She swayed and held onto him even tighter. It felt like she had fallen into a deep, warm pool, diving down and down until the whole, real world vanished somewhere high above. All she knew in that one dream-like moment was *him*. His touch, his kiss, the way he made her feel. So very alive.

It was better than any kiss she had ever read about. Better than anything she could have imagined.

She buried her fingers in the wavy silk of his hair, knocking his hat to the ground, and held him close to her. She felt him moan against her lips, a ragged sound of need that met hers in fiery rush. Their kiss turned even harder, more desperate...

Until a burst of laughter broke the hazy bubble of her sensual dream. She stumbled back from him until her back hit the wall of the summer house, and she glanced around frantically.

Luckily no one was near; the laughter came from a few women near the pond. But she could easily have been caught, a scandal flaring up in Mrs. Astor's garden, her job at the paper gone—her parents hearing about it. Yet somehow she couldn't really care. She could get addicted to that reckless feeling inside only Frank Markov created.

Especially when she looked up at him and saw the dark turmoil in his usually icy eyes.

"*Sumasshedshaya zhenshchina.*" He bent down, and for one crazy second she thought he would touch her foot. But he just scooped up his hat, and her notebook, which had tumbled from her hand to the ground.

Jessica snatched it out of his hand, suddenly remembering it had her jottings from Club 501 as well as notes from the garden party. "Th—thank you," she stammered.

He smiled down at her, and she could see the amusement in his face, the dark desire in his eyes that made them not the blue of ice but of a stormy sky. The desire that called out to her own and frightened her as much as she longed for it.

She had no idea what to do now. She only knew she had to get away from him, because with him so near she couldn't possibly think straight. "I—I must be going now," she stammered. "Thank you for a lovely walk, Mr. Markov."

She spun around and ran down the steps, sure she was acting like the deepest-dyed coward, but she couldn't help it. She didn't feel like herself at all when he was near.

"Miss Hatton, please! If I have offended..." he called after her.

Jessica made herself laugh. "Oh, no, no! Just me being silly. I have an appointment I must get to now. We'll see each soon I'm sure, at Club 501!"

She dashed away, not stopping until she was on a

bus headed for her flat, away from the rarefied world of the Astors and from the attractive enigma of Frank Markov. The taste of his kiss lingered on her lips, and her nerves hummed with the excitement and danger of it all. She had never been kissed at all before, not really! Fumblings in the shrubbery at Hatton Hall could never compare to the dark desires Frank awakened in her. Was she ready for that yet?

She drifted as if in a dream up the stairs to the flat, and as soon as she opened the door, her orchid-like fantasy bubble popped at the sound of raw, terrified sobbing.

Jessica dropped her hat and bag on the floor and ran into the sitting room, panicked at what she might find. Charli sat on their threadbare old sofa, her knees drawn up as she cried. Her spectacles were discarded, and her face was streaked with tears. She still wore her burgundy silk gown and apron from work and smelled of sweet scones. Whenever she started baking a lot, it was a sure sign something was amiss.

"Charli, darling, whatever has happened?" Jessica cried. She took her friend into her arms, and Charli sobbed against her shoulder. The whole fantasy scene in Mrs. Astor's summerhouse seemed so very far away.

"Last night, a—a lady was found in the alleyway behind Club 501! She was, oh Jess, she was *dead*! Murdered! It was so terrifying."

A dead woman behind Club 501—Frank Markov's speakeasy? Jessica suddenly felt ice cold, remembering how he walked with her in the gardens so insouciantly only an hour before. "Who was it? Not..." Oh, God. Not Meggie or Eliza. It couldn't be!

"I didn't know her, but I was so scared," Charli

said. "Oh, Jess! What's going to happen now?"

Jessica held on tight to Charli as she cried and wished she could answer her. There was absolutely no way to see what might happen next at a place like Club 501, with a man like Frank Markov. They could only hold on tight and follow the ride or get off altogether. And the latter was no longer an option.

****

"Glad you could make it today, Mr. Markov," Mr. Sheldon, a state senator and friend of Mr. Astor, said as Frank stepped back onto the terrace. Senator Sheldon passed him a cup of the "tea," the finest of bootlegged French brandy, as the low voices of the men hiding out from their wives flowed around them.

Frank studied the ladies who fluttered around the garden in their pale silks, but he didn't see Jessica there. He could still taste her, still feel her softness in his arms, and he damned himself as he realized he wanted her to be there again more than anything else.

Yet he couldn't be sorry for kissing her. It was the only minute he could forget, could feel light again, young. He wanted more of it, of her.

"I'm glad I could make it here, as well, Senator Sheldon," Frank said. "Your support for our plan has been vital."

The senator smiled, all wealthy satisfaction and self-assurance. "These Bolshies coming in here and causing trouble—it's bad for business. We can't have that. Especially not with the presidential election coming up so soon."

"No, indeed," Frank muttered, thinking of the senator's "business interests"—speakeasies and brothels, from New York all the way down to Florida.

Not very savory, but for now it played into his own interests.

"I've heard tell of some trouble down on the docks," the senator said with a frown. "Cocaine coming in from South America, girls kidnapped, that sort of thing. No one's been able to catch whoever's in charge yet. You think it's the reds?"

Frank thought of rumors he'd heard, of new gangsters coming from the Midwest, but nothing new about the anarchists. Most of them seemed far too disorganized to pull together such a business scheme. They were only interested in destroying things, just as they were in Russia. "I haven't heard whispers about it yet. It doesn't sound like a Bolshevik scheme, but they could be getting desperate. I'll ask around."

"Good, good. I knew we could count on you." The senator's attention fell on a pretty, apple-cheeked blonde in pink chiffon strolling past the terrace. He tipped his hat to her, and she giggled.

"No need for everything to be *all* business, though," the senator said. "You're a handsome young fellow, Mr. Markov, and everyone sure loves your new club. You should take advantage of that, have some fun."

Frank thought about Jessica and her kiss again, shocked at the way it wouldn't leave him. It was too distracting. He had to forget her. "I am too busy for *fun* right now."

Senator Sheldon gave a loud laugh. "A man should never be too busy for that! Take it from me—all work and no play makes a dull boy. It's cliché but true."

The senator wandered off to find his blonde, and Frank laughed before he drank down the last of the "tea." He was afraid Jessica Hatton's intense version of fun would make him useless for anything else, and that couldn't be. Not now.

Chapter Nine

Jessica stared across the street at the building
secretly housing Club 501. In daylight, it was even less
impressive than at night. The narrow alleyway snaked
away off the bustle and noise of Broadway, but it might
as well have been on a different planet. The car horns
and shrieks were muffled on the grimy brick walls, so
tall they cut off the daylight.

She leaned deeper into the recessed doorway,
trying to keep out of sight herself as she studied the
street. A cat streaked out from behind a trashcan, the
only sign of life in the strangely deserted-looking
buildings. In the light of day, the street was surely one
of the most silent, nondescript places in the whole city.
That was probably very good for Club 501's business.
Who would go looking for a sparkling, glamorous
nightclub *here*? But it all felt so sinister, with those
boarded windows on the lower floors and the smell of
mold and boiled cabbage in the still air.

Jessica shivered and peered cautiously down the
dark maw of the cracked stone stairs she knew led
down to the speakeasy. It was just as silent and deserted
as everything else in the workaday world here at the
surface, with windblown trash caught in the railings.
She saw no hint of any life at all there, but she knew
she wasn't quite brave enough to lurk there after night
fell. Not after what Charli told her.

Jessica had always been called a daredevil by her family, the subject of her mother's censorious sighs, her father's long-suffering glances, her siblings' teasing laughter. *Get Jess to do it, she'll try anything.* And she knew leaping before she looked had led her into plenty of trouble in the past. It had even led her here.

But she didn't want it to get her killed, that was for sure. She was young, there were too many more adventures out there. She glanced toward the end of the street, where there were glimpses of reassuring things like taxis and fruit trucks. For an instant, she considered running back there. Going home and writing up her safe little garden party story.

Remembering Mrs. Astor and her roses stiffened her resolve. Yes, there were lots of adventures left—but writing about hats forever wasn't one of them. Not if she really wanted to make a difference in the world. And wasn't that why she had come to New York?

"I'll just take one little peek," she told herself. She wrapped her coat, her oldest garment of nondescript brown wool, closer around her shoulders and strode off down the narrow street on her flat-heeled shoes. Out of long practice, she could pretend far more confidence that she actually felt.

She slipped between two of the tall, narrow buildings and found an even narrower alleyway that ran behind. That was where Charlotte said they found the poor woman's body, and Jessica could see signs of it. Police markers, already torn and trampled, fluttered between overturned trash bins, and cigarette butts littered the dirty pavement where officers had milled around. One shoe, a blue satin, beaded creation worn down at the heel, was casually discarded. A heartrending sight.

That shoe made Jessica feel even more angry. This was a dismal place to die, all alone and terrified. And the police were already gone. They surely didn't even care who had done the hideous crime. What was the loss of one more scared young woman in the big city?

But Jessica cared. She knew she had to help if she could. She hurried over to the trash bins, holding her breath against the pungent garbage smells. It looked like the rubbish had already been picked up, no clues left there.

She turned back to the buildings, counting until she knew which one of the identical brick structures housed Club 501. She remembered the long tunnel and hidden rooms. Surely it was used for smuggling in booze, and it had to come out somewhere. She paced the length of the alley but couldn't find anything suspicious at all. Frank Markov's people were obviously good at their illegal activities.

She remembered the room where the Russians were meeting and frowned at one window set in the dirty brick wall just above her head. She suspected it was the room above the tunnel. She hopped up and caught at the stone ledge, much as she had with the branches of trees when she was a schoolgirl. She pulled herself up until she found a toehold in the rough wall and could peer through the window.

It was streaked with grime and spider webs, and Jessica could scarcely see anything. She squinted and could just barely make out the outline of chairs and a table. And—was that a bed in the corner? She peered closer, but couldn't quite tell...

"Hey! What are you doing there?"

Jessica gasped at the sudden shout. Her precarious grip on the ledge slipped, and she tumbled back to the pavement. She barely managed to stay on her feet as the impact vibrated up her legs. She leaned against the support of the wall as she stared at one of the largest men she had ever seen.

Not large like Frank Markov, tall and lean and elegant, but *large*, with a belly hanging over his incongruously expensive wool trousers. Surely she had seen him somewhere before? He was so tall he blocked out the meager light from the end of the alley. He wore a bright purple waistcoat and a white hat with a matching purple band, which should have looked ludicrous.

But Jessica feared she couldn't laugh when she looked into his face and saw the scar that bisected his jowly check. The glitter of his narrow eyes.

An image of the dead girl who was found right in that alley flashed through her mind, and for the first time she felt a cold shiver of real fear wriggle through her. As usual, it was much too late for her to be prudent.

"What are you doing here, girlie?" he demanded roughly, his voice tinged with a flat, shrill accent. "Snooping around where you don't belong? Ain't a good idea in this city."

Jessica was beginning to figure that out. She couldn't keep herself from being "snoopy." Yet she *could* get out of there now.

Using the quickness honed on the field hockey grounds of Mrs. Greensley's School, she feinted left. When he grabbed for her, she went right and dashed around him in a wide circle. The alley was so narrow her sleeve scraped against the brick wall, slowing her down a fraction. He grabbed her in a bruising grip, yanking her around so hard she thought her shoulder was wrenched from its socket.

"Bloody bastard!" she shouted. She brought her foot down on his instep and ground her low heel into it. At the same time, she swung up her free hand and smashed the heel of her palm into his already-flattened nose.

"Bitch!" he cried through a gratifying squirt of blood from his nostrils. He slapped her across the face, snapping her head around, and she screamed as long and loud as her lungs would let her.

She managed to drive her elbow into that massive belly. His hold loosened enough that she could pull free. She started running, almost blind with panic. He let out a bellow and dove after her, only to be suddenly lifted back and away, as if by some magic force.

Shocked, Jessica spun around and pressed her back to the wall, just in time to see her assailant land in the grime of the walkway. He looked shocked, too, his eyes wide in his blood-streaked, porcine face. He tried to push himself up, but a fist landed in that face.

Jessica's stare flew up to find it was Frank Markov. He had seemingly appeared from nowhere to hook his arm around the pig-man's neck and fell him with one blow. He punched him again, and then once more, such quick blows they looked weirdly light and elegant. Yet they made the villain collapse back to the ground, his eyes rolling back in his head. His hat blew away down the alley.

Jessica could only stare, numb, until a hysterical laugh bubbled up inside of her. Frank spun around and stared at her, his eyes very dark blue.

"What are you doing here?" he demanded. His Russian accent was much heavier now. "Do you not know what has happened?"

"I..." For once, Jessica seemed to have lost her voice. She shook her head, trying to drive out that hazy, dream-like feeling. "Yes, that poor girl."

"Then what are you doing here alone? Are you *c yma*?"

Jessica didn't know much Russian, but she didn't much like the sound of that word. She drew herself up to her full, admittedly not very great, height and stared up at him. He looked so calm, so marble-still, with such dark, stormy eyes, she was even more afraid than when that terrible man grabbed her. "Just a minute there, mister..."

The felled giant at their feet groaned, and she fell back a step.

"There is no minute now. Come with me." Frank grabbed her hand and pulled her with him to the other end of the alley. She could only stumble after him. It wouldn't do to be left alone in the alley, after all.

He led her through a trapdoor she hadn't seen before, it was so closely disguised against the grimy wall. It reminded her of a priesthole at one of the neighboring manors at Hatton Hall, the old hiding place tucked snugly under a staircase. She hadn't liked going in there, either, even when Lulu dared her when they were kids. Dark and dank weren't much fun.

But now she knew it was either the trapdoor, or getting past Goliath, who was slowly groaning his way back to life. She followed Frank.

He pulled the door closed behind them, and she

saw they were in the underground passageway again. Most of the orange crates were gone, replaced by boxes marked "Milk," and two burly men were stacking them along the walls. One she recognized as Yevgeny, though mercifully his trousers were securely fastened today.

Frank said something to them in Russian and gestured to the alley outside. They nodded and hurried that way. Though they gave her curious looks as they passed, they said nothing to her. They vanished outside, no doubt to get rid of the man lolling around in the dirt.

How useful it must be to have burly minions, she thought.

She turned back to Frank and looked up at him in the dim, flickering light from the passage. He still had that stony, watchful air about him, and she felt herself almost mesmerized as she looked into his eyes.

"You're bleeding," he said roughly. Though his accent was still strong, he looked calmer, almost icy. "Right here." He slowly reached out to place a petal-light touch beside her lip.

Startled, Jessica reached up to feel her mouth. It seemed to tingle where his finger had pressed, and she suddenly remembered their kiss in every vivid, sizzling detail.

She didn't know which scared her more. Goliath out there or being alone with Frank in here.

"I didn't even realize. It must have split when that jerk out there hit me." She reached for her handkerchief, only to realize she had lost her handbag out in the alley. "Drat, I dropped my bag out there!"

"One of the boys will fetch it," Frank said. "Come, let's get you cleaned up, then I will drive you home."

"Oh, no," she said quickly. "I can take myself home now that you've so gallantly saved me. I don't want to be any more trouble." Nor did she want him to know what she was actually up to, looking for a story at Club 501.

For the first time that day, some of the ice around him seemed to crack. There was even a hint of a smile. "You shouldn't wander around New York like that unless you want to attract even more unwanted attention. From the police, for instance."

Jessica glanced down at herself, surprised to find she really was in a most disreputable state. Her skirt was streaked with dirt and mold, one coat sleeve ripped, and her bodice dotted with blood. Her hat was crooked, and no doubt her hair was tangled and her face grubby.

She gave a hysterical little laugh. "Mummy would have a fit."

"Then let's get you cleaned up before Mummy sees you."

Jessica's laugh turned full-blown. "No worries about that, anyway. She's an ocean away."

It seemed like there were plenty of other things to worry about, though. Especially the mysterious and all too wildly attractive man who now led her down the passageway.

They emerged into the main room of Club 501. It looked very different without the midnight crowds of revelers, large and shadowed, almost eerie.

The countess stood behind the bar, a ledger in one hand as she counted bottles. She looked just as elegant as ever in a pale green suit and cream silk blouse, her silvery hair brushed back from her face, but she also looked older, more tired. Not quite as glamorous, but surely just as fearsome.

She glanced up as Frank led Jessica to one of the tables near the empty dance floor. Her eyes widened, and her pencil went still, but she said nothing. Jessica wondered if such things happened every day at Club 501. Disheveled girls and burly Russians marching past on all kinds of errands.

"Jessica, this is my aunt, the Countess Markova," Frank said. "I fear Miss Hatton had a small mishap outside."

His *aunt*. So that was why he was talking to her so closely on the ship, why she was here now. Jessica didn't know why she was surprised, or relieved.

"So I see," Countess Markova said, a small smile touching her rouged lips. Jessica could see now the slight resemblance between her and Frank, in that wry, Slavic smile, the sculpted cheekbones. "I am sorry to hear that, Mademoiselle Hatton. One must always be so cautious in this wretched city, I fear. I will fetch some warm water and bandages, yes?"

She disappeared through that door behind the bar, and Frank took a bottle of French brandy from the shelf. He poured out two generous glasses and pressed one into Jessica's hand.

"My aunt is right, you know," he said, tossing back his own drink. "It's not safe for you to wander the city like you do."

Jessica took a long drink of the smooth amber liquid, relishing the warm bite of it. It seemed to bolster her with a fresh courage. "If I wanted to be wrapped up in cotton wool and put on the shelf like a porcelain doll, I would have stayed in England. I don't want to write about flower shows forever. I do want to write *real* stories, things that inform and help people. I want to be useful."

He smiled, and this time it looked different, more reluctant, more real. "Reading of things like flowers and parties *can* be useful, you know, Jessica. People always need lightness and beauty in their lives. It can make the darkness brighter, can remind of us of what we really fight for."

Jessica took another sip of brandy. She had never thought about it like that. "What do *you* fight for, Frank?"

He sat back in his chair, his expression a mask again. "Me? I fight for my own fortune, of course. What else does any man do in a place like this New York?"

She didn't believe him one bit. She had seen too much of what he tried to hide, his deep concentration and fierceness, the wistfulness of their dance and their kiss, to believe him. He hid something deep inside. "Did you know who that girl was? The one found in the alley?"

His expression darkened, and he poured out another measure of brandy. "*Nyet*. She may have been here before, but we get many ladies like her, who want to dance and have a drink, have some fun. I try to look out for my customers, but sometimes it is not possible. Whatever happened to her, it had nothing to do with my business operation here at Club 501. None of my associates knew her, either. But we will find out."

Jessica took another gulp of her drink. It was surely too fine to abuse like that, but it did bolster her courage. "Your associates? Much like Yevgeny and his friends?"

If he was surprised she knew Yevgeny's name, he

didn't show it. He just gave a faint smile. "Yevgeny was in the army with me once. He can be trusted. And he is good at discovering information rough sorts like your alleyway friend would prefer stay hidden."

Yevgeny had been in the army with Frank? Jessica turned that over in her mind, trying to picture it. "He doesn't look much like some White Russian army man."

"What makes you think I am White Russian?"

She laughed. "Oh, Frank. You might as well have 'aristocrat' stamped on your forehead. Your manners, your clothes, the way you walk and dance. I'm the daughter of an earl whose title goes back to Bosworth, but even my mother's pride has nothing on the Russian refugees I met in London."

He turned the glass in his hand, seemingly idle as he watched the liquid swirl. He finally nodded, as if he had decided something. "You are right, my lady reporter. My mother, my aunt's sister, was the granddaughter of Tsar Alexander II. My father was from the old nobility of Kiev, though he died when I was too young to know him. My mother took me to court with her when she would serve the Dowager Empress Marie, and we had a summer house in Livadia, near the royal family's palace. I suppose we *were* stamped aristocrat. Now I am a working man like any other."

Jessica was pretty sure he could *never* be like "any other" man anywhere. She was fascinated by his tale, hungry for more details he seemed reluctant to give.

The countess suddenly appeared in the doorway, a basin and a roll of bandages in her hands. Her beautiful face looked shocked. "Nicolai Dimitriovich, no! You mustn't speak of it, of them."

He gave his aunt a weary smile. "It is quite all right, aunt. Lady Jessica here is the daughter of an English earl. She is no Bolshevik spy."

"Bah!" The countess would surely have spat on the floor if she wasn't so very elegant. "The English king. He abandoned our tsar to his fate." She put the basin down on the table and soaked a cloth in the steaming water with quick, jerky movements. She pressed it to Jessica's lip, careful and gentle despite the angry fire in her eyes. "Do you know the king, then, *Lady* Jessica?"

"Not personally," Jessica said carefully around the cloth. "I saw him at my debut drawing room, with Queen Mary."

"And very grand they were, I'm sure. I hear the queen wears the tiara from our own dowager empress, bought with mere pennies." The countess dabbed a bit of salve onto Jessica's tiny wound. "My nephew here danced with the poor, doomed grand duchesses while their grandmother wore those very diamonds."

Jessica was too startled by her short words to answer, until the countess finished her chore and stalked away with the empty basin. "You danced with the grand duchesses?" she asked Frank. She remembered stories of those girls, their beauty and their merry spirits, cut off too soon. Like the girl in the alleyway.

"At Livadia, at the Grand Duchess Olga's debut ball. They were younger than me, but my mother instructed me that I must dance with them." He smiled faintly as if at the memory. "They were very pretty, but very innocent. Full of questions about the world outside their palaces. Full of laughter. Much like you, I would say, Lady Jessica."

"Were you in love with any of them?" she said, half-sad, half-teasing.

His smile widened. "They were as sheltered and watched over as a pink diamond, not like other girls were. And I was young and careless. So very, very careless. I didn't know what waited for us."

"Aren't all young men careless? They have so much freedom to be that way, unlike us girls," Jessica said. Though she remembered plenty of young men who were no longer careless at all. Men like her dear brother-in-law, scarred outside and in by the horrors of war. Like her brother Bill, who had never come back from battle.

Frank Markov had been in the war, too.

"Ah, yes," he said. "With our fast cars, and our whiskey and gambling. I thought that summer in Livadia was how life would always be. The white palace on the hill, the ocean in the moonlight, the pretty girls in their pink gowns."

Jessica was enchanted by the images his words conjured in her mind. "What happened to you then?"

He shrugged. "What happened to us all. I went off to battle. And those lovely girls died horrible deaths, with no one to save them. Now I'm here in New York, with a new life, just like you."

"Yes," Jessica murmured. "Just like me." Like so many people now who had to find new way to live, new ways to think.

Frank suddenly reached out and touched her cheek with his fingertips, so light and soft she thought she imagined it. Her gaze flew up to meet his, startled, to find his eyes the pale blue of summer again.

"You do remind me something of them, Jessica," he said. "That sweet, eager innocence, that curiosity that drives you to run out and see all the lovely things you're sure the world has waiting. I hope that never changes for you."

Jessica could almost think he was right when she looked into those eyes, but she knew the world held plenty of ugliness to discover, too. "I know the world isn't always so lovely."

"No. But you do seem determined to make it so." For an instance, she glimpsed something in the depth of his eyes she thought was like—longing. But then in a flash it was gone. He gave her one of his careless smiles and turned away.

She watched as he put away the brandy, wishing he would talk to her more, share more of his hidden self with her. But that seemed very unlikely to happen now.

"Are you feeling better?" he asked. "Shall I see you home?"

She smiled back at him, bright and quick. She was bloody well not going to show him how she felt inside. She didn't even *know* how she really felt now. Everything seemed so upside-down.

"Right as rain," she said. "I can take the bus home. You should be getting ready to open up here for the night, right?"

"There's plenty of time," he said. He glanced at the hidden door.

Suddenly, Jessica remembered everything that had happened that day. The reason she was sitting here with torn stockings and a busted lip. She'd been too caught up in mooning over Frank Markov and his romantic, tragic past to even think about who that nasty bully outside could be. Some reporter she had turned out to be.

Whoever he was, surely Frank wanted to talk to his men and make sure he was gone. And she had a lot to think about indeed.

She definitely couldn't think straight when Frank was around.

"I've already been enough trouble today," she said firmly. "I've got to get home and get changed myself, for a—a date."

"A date?" he asked doubtfully, almost as if he wasn't sure what the word meant. He looked at her closely.

She smiled even wider, until her wounded lip hurt.

Finally, he nodded. "I will see you into a taxi. You are surely in no state for buses. If you don't want me to stay with you any longer."

She nodded, just wanting to be out of there and back to the flat as soon as possible. If she was lucky, she would get there and cleaned up before anyone else saw her.

Frank gently took her arm and helped her out to the street. He even fetched a taxi off Broadway so she wouldn't have to walk any further. As he paid the driver, Jessica glanced up at the building that hid Club 501. She glimpsed his aunt at one of the upstairs windows, staring down at them, her face pale behind the glass.

The taxi zoomed off through the city, the sky already turning the palest of pinks above the buildings as the day closed. It was only when she opened the door to her own, blessedly empty flat that she remembered her handbag was still at Club 501. With her notebook still inside of it.

****

The handbag was a shimmering, flashing beaded beacon in the daytime shadows of the alley outside Club 501—just as Jessica Hatton seemed to have become in the gloom of the everyday world of his life. Her laughter, her curiosity, her willingness to jump ahead no matter what, showed him just how old and hardened he had become. She made him want to laugh again, too, despite everything.

Frank shook his head ruefully. He had become so poetical over a lady who was proving to be an energetic bundle of trouble—right when he didn't need any more trouble at all.

He stooped to pick up the purse that had fallen to the floor under Jessica's chair. It was large, black satin sewn with black and silver beads in a flowered pattern. The beaded clasp had come undone, and as he refastened it he glimpsed a notebook falling out of its depths amid lipstick tubes and enameled compacts.

Curious, he pulled it out and examined the blue leather-bound volume. It was stamped in gold letters on the cover, JEOH surmounted with a little coronet. A small gold pencil was attached to the spine with a length of satin ribbon. A very expensive, elegant little book. But the notes jotted inside were hurried, slapdash, dotted with several question marks and exclamation points.

Frank had intended only to glance at it and then tuck it behind the bar until he could return it to its owner, but one of the pages caught his attention. Notes about the missing girl who had been found in the alley, along with far too many questions. Was she planning a story about the sad murder?

"*Durak*!" he cursed. The lady was surely a danger to herself, chasing such things around the city, getting mixed up with the darkness that lurked around every corner. He had to stop her, for her own good.

"Has she gone?" he heard his aunt say.

He glanced back to see her emerging from the back room, her calm mask in place again. "*Da.* You know I sent her home in a taxi."

"She should be more careful, the silly English lady. She does not know what she is doing here."

"Do any of us?" he said quietly.

His aunt shook her head. "She reminds me too much of myself when I was that age," she muttered. She went to clean up the basin and bandages left on the table. "Much too reckless."

He smiled at her, thinking of the tales his mother once told him of the days she and her sister were young, of the trouble his aunt would lead them into.

He gave her a smile. "You ended up on your feet, though, *uika*."

"Cheeky boy. I suppose I did, or will do so soon, once our work here is done." She left her basin and towels and came to stand by him at the bar. "But she could get herself, and all of us, into much trouble. We are so close now..."

Frank nodded, thinking of their scheme to catch some of the Bolsheviks who tried to infiltrate New York as they had his homeland, using their own criminal bootlegging activities to snare them. "Don't worry, *uika*," he said. "I will see to it that neither Lady Jessica, nor any other innocent, will get into any trouble."

Even if she seemed determined to dive headlong into nothing *but* trouble, the maddening, beautiful girl.

Chapter Ten

"I'm glad you're going with me tonight, Jess," Meggie said in the back of the taxi as they sped through the nighttime city on their way back to Club 501. She squeezed Jessica's hand and gave a grin, but Jessica could see the shadow at the back of her friend's eyes. The grim news of the girl in the alleyway had even affected stout-hearted Meggie.

Jessica smiled back. She knew Meggie would never want anyone to see her fright. Jessica didn't want anyone to see her own. "I have to get my handbag back, don't I?" And make sure no one read that notebook.

"How did you lose it, anyway?" Meggie asked. "You didn't say."

"It must have fallen off my arm while I was dancing there," Jessica answered lightly. "Wickedly careless of me, I know. At least there wasn't much money in it."

The taxi let them off at the end of the alley, and Jessica and Meggie made their way down the walkway, talking and laughing loudly all the way. Luckily, they weren't the only ones there. Even though it was relatively early in the evening, there was already a short line at the underground stairs, elegantly dressed couples and a group of tiddly young men in silk hats and expensive jackets.

It seemed a murder wasn't going to slow down

business. In fact, it increased it.

Tiny the doorman recognized Meggie and let them in right away. Inside, it wasn't quite as crowded yet, not so many dancers flowing around the floor. Jessica studied the people who were there, but Frank Markov and his aunt were nowhere to be seen.

Meggie made her way to the stage, where the band was still warming up, and Jessica went to the bar. Ira the bartender was making up a row of glowing magenta-pink cocktails, but he glanced up at her with a smile, never spilling a precious drop of gin.

"What'll it be tonight, then, miss?"

"One of those yummy things with the pomegranate again, I think," Jessica said with what she hoped was an innocent smile. "And I think I left my handbag here. I guess no one would have turned it in?"

He laughed. "We're more honest than you might think." He reached down on a shelf behind the bar and came up with her beaded bag, swinging on its fringed handle. "The boss himself gave it to me. Said he thought you might be looking for it."

Jessica felt her cheeks turn warm in a blush. "Thanks. I guess I owe him." She took her drink and turned to look at the room again. It was starting to fill up as the line moved inside, becoming noisier with the trays of drinks circulating. Meggie was launching into her first song.

Jessica barely had time to take a sip of the delicious drink when there was suddenly a huge crash. She reacted instinctively, her heart pounding as she ducked.

She peeked up to see that the front door was broken open, shattered and splintered, and blue-uniformed cops spilled inside. Jessica looked around frantically as the crowd screamed and scattered, but she couldn't see Meggie in the pandemonium.

"This is a raid!" a policeman shouted. "Everyone put their hands up! Now!"

His words didn't calm the panic. Jessica pressed herself against the bar, trying to keep from being mowed over by the flood of people stampeding toward the doors. The bartender suddenly grabbed her around the shoulders and forcibly lifted her up over the abandoned bar.

"This way!" he yelled over the cacophony. She ran behind him through the hidden door into the tunnel. Their escape path was horribly blocked by more blue uniforms pouring in off the alley. People in dinner jackets and sparkling gowns were being herded in front of them, a few escaping around the corner.

Jessica had a sudden, intriguing glimpse of two of the men she had seen in the tunnel that night she overheard Frank talking in Russian. They were being hauled into a police truck, shouting Russian curse words. She didn't have time to think much about them, though, since she was cornered herself.

Ira just groaned and held up his hands. From the stories of raids, Jessica was expecting far more drama and danger. But the cops just pushed the bartender a little when he was too slow going out the door. The cop who took Jessica's arm, a young, smooth-shaven chap with soft brown eyes under his helmet, gave her an apologetic smile.

"Sorry, miss," he said. "Y—you're arrested for—for imbibing."

He didn't even put her in handcuffs, just led her out

of the building to where another black police truck waited. Now that the initial rush of raw panic had gone, Jessica looked around for possible interesting details to put in a story, but it was all shockingly mundane. It looked like most of the patrons had escaped or bribed their way free. She saw the musicians with their instruments herded past, but no Meggie. She also wasn't among the sobbing or bored women around Jessica, which made her hope Meggie had escaped.

The ride in the truck was also disappointingly dull. An older woman next to Jessica complained loudly, while a girl in too much rouge sobbed until her makeup ran. Jessica offered her a handkerchief, which she seized in a hard grasp. She proceeded to tell Jessica all about her "chump" boyfriend George who had ungallantly abandoned her in the raid.

When they were led into a holding cell, Jessica and the now much more cheery rouged girl were fast friends, and Jessica had even learned a few valuable makeup tips from her. The cell itself had a few possibilities for atmosphere in a story. The stark gray stone walls and floor, the hard benches the sparkling-gowned women perched on, the sharp smell of disinfectant and perfume—very dramatic. They were led out one by one to make their phone calls. They started out with ten ladies, the ones unlucky enough to not be able to escape the raid, but slowly it dwindled until there was only Jessica and two others, one of the women drunk and sobbing, the other almost nodding asleep as they waited for their husbands to bail them out.

By the time Jessica's new friend was taken away by her stern-faced mother, she was alone. The quiet let the first hints of worry seep in. She had no money on her for bail, and no idea who to call. They had no phone in the flat, and she didn't know where Eliza and Charlotte could be. Did Meggie get away, or was she also locked in a cell somewhere? And, most important, where was Frank? Was he in terrible trouble after what happened at Club 501? Was he involved in the "red menace," and that was what led to the raid in the first place? The thoughts swirling around in her mind made Jessica jump up and pace the length of the cold, stone cell.

The door suddenly open again, and the portly sergeant who had been leading the women to the phone reappeared.

"Your turn, miss," he said, gesturing to Jessica, even though obviously there was no one else there. "You're sprung."

Sprung? Was that one of those strange American phrases she hadn't quite mastered yet? Did it mean "free"? Jessica studied his red face, puzzled. But she really didn't want to wait around to see if it was all a mistake. She hurried after the sergeant, wondering if somehow Meggie had shown up to rescue her. Or maybe, possibly, could it be Frank? Here to explain and laugh away what had happened?

But it wasn't Meggie, or Frank, who waited at the front desk. It was Frank's aunt, the forbiddingly elegant countess, who stood there in a lace-trimmed black pagoda coat, her face as disdainful and calm as if the grubby jail around her didn't even exist.

Her eyes, the same pale, penetrating blue as Frank's, swept over Jessica with no expression at all. "*Da*," she said. "This is her."

****

"Thank you for bailing me out," Jessica ventured to say as the taxi crawled along the crowded street. The silence since they left the police station had become almost deafening, broken only by the blare of car horns from beyond their windows, the laughter of the people who still crowded the sidewalks at two in the morning.

The countess sat next to her, a sphinx in a diamond-pinned turban, faintly smiling as bars of mottled streetlamp light fell across her face. Jessica could glimpse a distinct resemblance to Frank in the stark, aristocratic lines of her cheekbones, the glow in her eyes.

"I fear you were not meant to be caught up in that, Mademoiselle Hatton," the countess said calmly.

"Caught?" Jessica said.

The countess turned to look at her at last, a faint smile on her lips. "Surely a lady like yourself, a newspaper writer, could see that was not a *true* raid?"

Jessica frowned as she thought of other speakeasy raids she had read about, stock destroyed and customers beaten down and arrested, mostly because someone had forgotten to line the right pockets or had changed their distributor without taking the proper precautions. The raid on Club 501 had been oddly—businesslike, now that she thought about it. The Russian men in the back room, the girl in the alley... "Are you saying that Frank..."

"Frank. Yes," the countess said with a laugh. "He would never have let such a thing happen to you. He would have come himself at once when he learned you were in jail, but I insisted he let me do it. He has so much to finish tonight, you see. So much we have been working toward for so long."

Jessica's thoughts were racing. She had always known there was more to Frank than he wanted to meet the eye. But what had really happened tonight? She *had* to make the countess tell her, had to know the truth at last. She was tired of feeling as if she merely flailed around in the dark, half-seeing glimpses of the truth, unable to piece it all together. "What exactly did happen tonight, madame? I know Frank has been through a great deal with the war, but Club 501..."

The countess shocked Jessica by suddenly reaching out to touch her hand. Her skin was cool, her heavy ring imprinted with a gold double-eagle on a cabochon sapphire. "Frank will tell you everything, my dear, I am sure. I can see that you will not rest until you know. I was once so much like you."

"How so, madame?"

"When I was young, I was quite the despair of my parents," the countess said with a grimace. "I wanted to rush out headlong to meet life, so sure great adventures waited for me out there. I danced all night, at grand balls and gypsy restaurants, rode my horse all day in the summer, drove my own sleigh in the winter, flirted with every handsome officer I met. My sister was the good one, the sweet one, the obedient one. I fear I drew her into so much trouble, which she would never have sought on her own."

Jessica was fascinated by this glimpse at the past of the remote, elegant countess, the flash of a real person beneath, a person who could help her understand Frank. "What happened?"

The countess looked away. "The revolution happened, of course. My husband had died in the war, and my sister was long widowed, raising her dear son all on her own. Frank, too, was at the front when it all happened. When the world exploded around us. Our elderly parents were killed in their own home, and I took my sister and ran. Frank fought his way back to us, found us where we were hiding in the Crimea. He saved my life, my brave nephew."

Jessica swallowed hard, fearful of what happened next. Where this tale was going. "And your sister?"

The countess's eyes grew shadowed, distant. "Olga was always so fragile. Beautiful and so sweet, but not like us, Mademoiselle Hatton. Life was not an adventure for my dear sister. She became ill with a fever, and there was no medicine, no food. She died before Frank could reach us. He has been seeking to right that terrible wrong ever since, to revenge her death, the loss of our home."

The countess fell silent, staring out at the city night with her pale, powdered face as still as a marble statue. Jessica was absolutely certain that wasn't the end of the tale, but it was obvious the countess would say no more now.

As she had said—Frank had to be the one to tell it. If Jessica could persuade him. She thought of his icy eyes, the silent strength of him, and doubted she could do it. But she had to try.

She glanced out her own window. The buildings were growing darker now as they neared her own flat, the streets a little quieter, but the city was still alive, as it always was. Alive and new and vital, in a way England wasn't. But England was her home, and to know it was still there, waiting for her when she wanted it back, was everything. What if that home, that world, was violently snatched away, her family destroyed?

The countess was right. She had always seen life as an adventure, always something new and fascinating around every corner. But that was with the comfort of her family always waiting there. She'd seen enough new things in New York, heard enough sad tales, to know so very many adventures went horribly wrong. People always needed compassion and help—just as Frank's mother and aunt had when they lost their home so horribly.

Maybe her job at the newspaper was not uncovering crimes. It was telling the stories of the innocent people who were hurt by such evil in the world, whose lives were torn apart and who needed help. Like that poor murdered girl in the alleyway. Like Eliza. Like the countess and her fragile sister, and the young nephew who tried to save them and tried to somehow avenge them now.

She did not know Frank's whole story yet. But she would. Soon.

The taxi stopped outside her building, and Meggie came racing down the fire escape stairs before Jessica could think any more. She reached out to open the door, and the countess laid a gentle hand on her arm just for an instant.

"I beg you, my dear," the countess said, her Russian accent strong. "Be very careful. Adventure is not always what you expect it to be."

Chapter Eleven

Jessica pounded as hard as she could on the door to Club 501. It had already been repaired since the raid just last night, with boards nailed over the splintered holes, and everything seemed even quieter than before. But she was determined to get in.

"Frank!" she called. She pounded on the door again. "I know you must be there."

She certainly didn't *know* anything of the sort. He could be gone off to Fiji now for all she knew, his work in New York—whatever it really was—done. But something told her he still had more to do in New York, just as she did.

She glanced down at the newspaper in her hand. *Red Menace Ring Broken!* So that was what the raid on Club 501 was really all about. Breaking up a Bolshevik ring attempting to get a revolutionary toehold in America through bootlegging. She'd been tiptoeing on top of a big crime story all the time, and the fact that she hadn't realized it made her see she really wasn't cut out to be a big-time investigative journalist.

Yet she couldn't regret the realization, nor could she regret not pursuing such a story. What if she had slipped up and ruined it, let those men get away? The men whose sort had caused the destruction of Frank's family and home.

No, she had other stories to tell now. But first she

had to find Frank.

She reached out to pound on the door again and almost lurched into a fall as it suddenly swung open. She stumbled and pushed herself upright again, tilting back her hat to see Frank standing right in front of her.

He looked unsurprisingly as if he hadn't slept in a very long time, his beard dark along his sculpted jaw, dressed in his shirtsleeves.

"You shouldn't be here," he said tonelessly, his arms crossed over his chest. "I wouldn't think you would want to be, after last night."

"I—I wanted to thank you for sending your aunt to fetch me home," Jessica said.

"You wouldn't have needed rescuing in the first place, if not for me," he said.

Jessica made herself laugh, as if she had no idea what he spoke of. "Oh, no! It was very exciting. I'm just sorry that—well, that I got in the way of something very important. If I had known..."

"You would have written a story about it?"

She studied his hooded blue gaze carefully. He still watched her with no expression at all, but she thought she saw something flicker deep in that stare. Impatience? Anger? Yes, a story had been what she intended at first, but certainly not now. She felt guilty, unsure.

"I'm sorry," she said simply. "Your aunt did say I was much too apt to leap into adventure without looking."

A reluctant little smile quirked the corner of Frank's lips, which Jessica chose to consider a good sign. "My aunt said that, did she?"

"She said she was once like me, before..." Before

the war and revolution that drove the Markovs out of their home. She fell silent, for once completely without words.

"You should come in," Frank said, standing back to let her pass finally. Jessica hurried inside before he could change his mind.

The room had been hastily tidied up, broken chairs piled on tables that were pushed against the walls, trash swept into piles. The jewel-like array of liquor bottles were gone, and the air seemed stale and dusty. The silence without music and laughter was echoing.

Frank righted a stool by the bar for her to sit down, and fetched her a glass of the lovely amber-colored brandy.

"I saved one bottle," he said with a wry smile.

Jessica tossed the steadying, warming draught back before she could lose courage and run out of there. "What's your real name?"

His hand went still on the bottle. "Prince Nicolai Dimitrovich Romanov-Markov."

"Wow," Jessica sighed. "A prince."

"Just one of dozens of descendants of old Tsar Alexander. The title never meant much, even in Russia."

"But you danced with the grand duchesses."

"So I did. In another life."

Jessica swallowed hard, remembering the stark pain in the countess's few words, the realization of how it would feel to lose all she loved. "I am sorry, Frank. Your aunt told me some of what happened, of what you were trying to do here..."

Anger flashed across his face. "She should not have done that. She shouldn't have involved you in this at all. If they hadn't moved up the time of the raid so suddenly, I would have made sure you weren't here at all."

"Oh, no! I'm glad she told me," Jessica cried. "I want to know more about you. I want to help, if I can."

"No one can help now, I'm afraid. Those men who would have brought their brand of terror and destruction to America are behind bars now, but there will be more like them. My mother's suffering will never really be avenged."

"Then let me help! Let me write her story, the story of your family. It will make other people want to help, too."

Frank gave a sad smile and reached out to gently touch Jessica's face. She tried to hold him with her, but he drew back too soon. "Sweet Lady Jessica. Always so enthusiastic. So eager to help."

"I know sometimes I am *too* eager. My mother and sister always tell me so. But this time..."

Frank shook his head. "No, Jessica. You can't help. You should go home now. In fact, you should go back to England, where you would be safe. Even from yourself."

He turned away from her and reached for a rag to polish at the bar. Jessica suddenly felt a burning flash of anger that he could turn from her like that when she wanted so much to be with him. She started to shout out to him, to beg him to listen to her. But she'd seen her parents turn away from her in disinterest too many times to miss the signs of it now. She knew he wouldn't listen to her, no matter how she tried to persuade him. How she begged.

But she was Lady Jessica Hatton, no matter how

she kicked and squirmed at the title, at her true place in life. She wouldn't beg, not for anything. Not even for this man, who she knew she cared for too much.

She spun around and ran out of Club 501 before her anger could fade and the tears could start.

****

Red Menace Caught In Bootlegging Raid!

Frank frowned grimly down at the newspaper and ground out his cigarette in an empty wine glass on the bar. The reporters had done their work fast. He would almost have suspected the pen of Lady Jessica—if he didn't know for sure she hadn't gone home. She was angry at him for hiding the truth from her, letting her go to jail, but that had surely been the safest place for her while all the loose ends at Club 501 were tied up.

He studied the mess of the club, the overturned tables and glasses. The Russian revolutionary band who had been raising money by bootlegging had been caught in the raid, just as planned, but there was still work to do. Still villains out there. Including whoever had killed the girl and left her body in the alley, and Frank intended to do all he could to find out who that was.

No one in the New York shadow-world knew how deliberate the raid had been. Frank and the police had been careful to keep it that way. As far as anyone knew, it had been a raid like any other, and they happened all the time. New clubs popped up out of the old right away, and as soon as it could be cleaned up Club 501 would reopen. In the meantime, he would manage a friend's club around the corner, L'Argent d'Or—and thus keep up his contacts.

He just hoped he could keep Jessica Hatton out of

trouble now.

There was a loud pounding at the boarded-up door, and Frank reached for his pistol. But he quickly realized it wouldn't be needed right then.

"Mr. Markov!" a familiar woman's voice shouted. "I know you're in there. Let me in right now."

It was Jessica's friend, the singer Lady Margaret. Frank put away the gun and went to open the door.

He could see right away why the two women were friends. They had the same stubborn, angry light in their eyes, the same posture of standing with hands on hips. Lady Margaret glared at him as she swept past into the abandoned club.

"Can I fetch you a drink, my lady?" he asked, shutting the door.

"Of course not. I just had to come tell you what a cad you are for letting my friend sit in jail all night. And here I thought we all liked you!"

Frank almost laughed, but he knew better than to do that when faced with a lady's wrath. "It was for her own good. She could have been trapped here while the police rounded up a very dangerous gang. I couldn't bear to see that happen."

Lady Margaret bit her lip uncertainly. "The Bolshies, you mean?"

"Exactly. I knew my aunt would have her out of that cell in no time, but I am sure she would have stayed here to get a story and would have gotten into much trouble."

"Of course she would have wanted a story like that! But I still think you deserve a ticking-off for letting her be hauled away like that."

"Consider me—ticked off, then, Lady Margaret. I

promise you nothing like that will happen in the future, and I will do my very best to make it up to Lady Jessica. If she will let me."

Lady Margaret looked a bit mollified. She swept past him to sit down at one of the barstools. "I think I will have that drink now, thanks. And I also think I might know of a way you can make it up to her—or start to, anyway."

"I would love to hear it, then," Frank said. He went behind the bar and poured her out a generous measure of the rescued brandy. "I will do anything to make it up to her."

Lady Margaret nodded. "You do know that the usual stuff, flowers and jewelry and candy, won't work with Jess."

"I did suspect that, yes. She cannot be so easy as all that."

"Right. But you're working at L'Argent d'Or for a while, yes?"

"I see news travels fast."

"Around here it does." She took a deep sip of her drink and smiled. "I just so happen to have a one-night engagement coming up there, but Jess doesn't know it yet. Maybe we could devise a way to make a special evening for her..."

Chapter Twelve

"So you think it's a good story? You could use it?" Jessica asked. She leaned across the desk toward Mr. Thorpe, the editor of the *World*, and carefully studied his expression as he looked down at her notebook.

For once, he was actually smiling instead of looking like he was going to explode at any second. "Absolutely, Miss Hatton. Our readers love things like this—romantic stories, lost loves, sadness, triumph. Something to tug at the heartstrings, y'know? I'm sure they like to think they see themselves in these true-life tales. And it's certainly different from anything any other papers are doing right now."

Jessica smiled. She felt so many emotions flying through her—doubt, gratitude, hope. Maybe, just maybe, if Frank could see this he would understand and forgive her. "Thank you, Mr. Thorpe. I wasn't sure if it was really important enough."

"Important?" Mr. Thorpe looked down at the notes again, beaming.

"Yes. Like stories about crime and corruption, things like that," Jessica said. She cringed to remember how foolish she was when she first came to New York, so sure she could do anything, so sure she *knew* everything. In reality, she was just beginning to learn.

He gave a wry laugh. "Oh, Miss Hatton. Any two-bit hack in a cheap fedora can write sensational stories about crime and corruption. Stuff like that practically writes itself. But you—you're a storyteller, young lady. You can make readers care. Make them want to know more, to even want to help out. That's not so easy to find. It's just what I need more of here."

"Really?" Jessica said, still amazed. "So you think I should finish this story?"

"As fast as you can. Maybe even make it a series, interview some more people like this. 'New Faces of New York,' something like that."

"A series? I could certainly do that." Jessica thought of all the people she had met in New York, their Italian neighbors at the flat, the bartender at Club 501, Yevgeny. Surely they all had tales to tell.

And she also needed to tell the stories of women like the poor girl who had been found behind Club 501, whose tale was still unknown. She had lots of work ahead of her. Her next stop was surely the archives again.

Mr. Thorpe sat back in his chair, giving her a smug smile. "Then get to work, Miss Hatton! No more garden parties or fashion shows until you're done. And don't forget who discovered you, either."

Jessica hurried out of his office, her notes clutched in her hand. She barely heard the clatter of the typewriters or the shouts of the reporters; she was sure she must be floating off the linoleum floor. Her own series! Something to *really* write.

In the taxi on her way home, she studied all the people and buildings that flew past, every one of them full of ideas. Full of stories. What a wondrous place the city was, she thought. So new and exciting, so dangerous. So filled with the possibility of new beginnings.

And of endings. There were those, too.

Frank Markov's face flashed in her mind, for the millionth time since she had last seen him, days ago. Club 501 was closed now, and Meggie had a new job at a place called L'Argent d'Or, as well as a part in a new musical. Charli was baking, with a real job at a patisserie serving fine ladies lunches. Eliza spent more and more time away from the flat, becoming quieter and quieter. No one knew where Frank had gone, and Jessica knew because she had asked at every saloon she could find.

She had seen the headlines. The "Red Menace" gang had been captured that night of the raid on Club 501, just as the countess said was meant to happen. The mystery of the girl in the alleyway was still unsolved, though. It made her worry about Frank all the more.

Where *was* he? Had she come so far, finally started to realize her dream, only to lose something equally precious? There had to be a way to find him. Someplace she hadn't looked yet. She even had the wild idea that maybe her story was the way to find him. One of her interview subjects would know him, or he would read her fine words and realize he shouldn't have left...

She laughed at herself. It seemed her foolish idealism wasn't gone after all.

"This the place, miss?" the taxi driver asked, startling her out of her daydreams.

She looked up to find she was already back at the boarding house, the building quiet in the middle of the day. She quickly paid the driver and slid out of the car, eager to start her story and her search for Frank.

Only to freeze at the bizarre sight that greeted her. Standing on the grimy stoop was her mother and her sister Lulu, still wearing their travel coats and cloche hats as if they had come straight from the ship. They whispered together, studying the front door with its peeling paint and cracked window uncertainly.

But other than that they looked exactly as they had when Jessica left England. Her mother regal and elegant, her strand of pearls in place around her neck, Lulu so sweet and concerned. It was dream-like, amazing. And Jessica felt the warmest, most urgent surge of love wash over her. She hadn't realized how very much she missed them, needed them, until that moment.

"Jess!" Lulu cried. She raced down the steps and grabbed Jessica in her arms. She smelled like Joy perfume, all rose and jasmine, just like their shared sitting room at home. She smelled safe. "You really *are* here. Oh, thank goodness. How I've missed you, darling!"

"Thank goodness, indeed," Lady Hatton said gruffly. Jessica peeked up from Lulu's shoulder to see the countess coming toward them at a more dignified pace down the steps. She didn't smile; in fact, her face did not move at all, but her eyes were wide and suspiciously shiny. "You gave us quite the fright, young lady. Whatever do you mean by coming all the way to New York by yourself? It is not done, you know, not done at all."

"I—I'm sorry, Mama," Jessica stammered, feeling like she had just been dropped back in the nursery. "I know I should not have run away. But I was so desperate to write, you see. I couldn't think of anything else!"

"And you could not write at Hatton Hall? Do we not have ink and paper there?" Lady Hatton said. "My silly, dramatic Jessica. How we have missed you. You are not allowed to do such a thing to us again, not if I have to lock you in the south tower until you marry."

Jessica choked on a laugh. "Oh, Mama. Marrying one of those silly London boys was the last thing I wanted."

"Well. We shall see about that." And that was the last thing Lady Hatton said before she took Jessica into her arms and held onto her very tightly. Jessica hung on in turn, wanting to cry.

"Oh, Mama," she whispered. "I have missed you, too."

****

"And you live *here*? All four of you?" Lady Hatton demanded.

Jessica poured out the tea and passed cups to her mother and Lulu. She glanced at Meggie over their heads and had to bite back a giggle as Meggie made a hideous face. She wanted her mother to think life in New York was perfectly respectable and safe, so they wouldn't drag her back to England. But she could see that was probably a vain hope.

"Oh, yes, Mummy," Jessica said. "It's all quite comfortable. Would you care for a cake?" She held out a plate with some of Charli's sweet creations laid out in an enticing array.

Lady Hatton looked at them down her nose. "Are they bought from one of those hideous American grocery stores?"

"Certainly not. Charlotte made them. You

remember Charlotte, don't you?" Jessica said. "She wants to be a pastry chef."

"Does she indeed? I would have thought she at least would have more sense." Lady Hatton took a tiny bite of a lemon cake and studied the sitting room around them. Luckily Meggie had time to throw blankets over most of the mess before anyone came upstairs. "Well, you cannot stay here, of course. None of you girls can."

Panic rushed through Jessica. "Mummy..."

"No, Jessica, let me finish." Lady Hatton put down her cake and gave Jessica another stern stare. "I have had a great deal of time to think about all of this since you left us so precipitously. And Louisa counseled me on the ship. She told me some things I fear I did not know."

"Counseled?" Jessica said, confused. She glanced at her sister, who gave her a reassuring smile.

"I told Mother about your work," Lulu said, "and how important it was to you."

"Your father and I have always wanted what was best for our daughters," Lady Hatton said with a sigh. "But I fear we cannot quite decipher what that is. Perhaps we have been too strict since Bill died. You seemed miserable during your Season, and then when you ran away..."

A tear shimmered in Lady Hatton's eye, and Jessica became even more concerned. Her mother *never* cried! "Mummy, I never meant..."

Lady Hatton waved away Jessica's frantic words with her bejeweled hand. "Louisa tells me you have always wanted to write, and now you have some sort of job here doing just that. At some—some *newspaper*."

She made "newspaper" sound like "brothel." "It's quite a respectable office, Mummy. I've been writing about things like Mrs. Astor's rose garden. And I've met people like a Russian grand duke." She didn't think it was necessary to mention the whole crime reporting thing. Or the fact that Frank was, in fact not a grand duke, only a prince, and had been an undercover bootlegger.

"Be that as it may, I still do not like it," Lady Hatton said. "English ladies should find suitable husbands and manage fine homes. But I have no desire to see you miserable, Jessica. If what you want is to stay in America and write, you may do so for a while. Provided you let me move you and your friends into a safer apartment and you write to us every week. No more running off like a hoyden."

Her mother was actually letting her stay in America? Jessica hardly dared let herself believe it. She leaped out of her chair and threw her arms around her mother and sister. "Oh, you won't be sorry, I promise! Just wait until you read my stories. You'll see that it's right for me to be here now."

Lady Hatton carefully patted her hand, back to her usual stern self. "It is only for a short time, Jessica, then you must come home again. Now, I am in need of a rest. Louisa and I will go to our hotel, and we expect you to join us for dinner tonight so we can go over your plans."

Jessica saw them off, still feeling giddy, as if she had drunk too much champagne and then spun around and around until she fell. Had that truly just happened? Could she really stay in New York with her family's blessing? Even if it was for a while, it would give her time to prove herself...

And time to find Frank again. The Prince Nicolai Dimitriovich Romanov-Markov had not seen the last of her, no matter what he might think.

Chapter Thirteen

"Jessica, my dear, I am not at all sure this is a good idea," Lady Hatton said with a sniff as she followed Jessica and Lulu down a winding, dark staircase. They could hear the blast of a trumpet, the beat of a drum, the patter of dancing steps and laughter.

"Oh, Mummy," Lulu said, straightening her beaded headband. "It will be fun! You said yourself we should see something of New York before we go home."

"I was thinking of the shops on Fifth Avenue, perhaps the Statue of Liberty," Lady Hatton said. She drew her satin wrap closer around her as they stepped into the main room of L'Argent d'Or, which Meggie said they had to see. It sparkled like its name, gleaming with gilt everywhere, on delicate French chairs and prancing cupids on marble stands.

"You can see all that tomorrow, Mama," Jessica said. "Won't it be thrilling to tell your friends you saw a real American speakeasy?"

"It would be a scandal," Lady Hatton muttered.

"Every family needs a scandal once in a while," Lulu said.

"Surely we have you and Jessica for that."

Lulu laughed and took her mother's arm as they made their way into the sparkling golden crowd. It was all brighter than Club 501, bigger, gaudier, but just as fun. Jessica recognized several of the regulars from

Club 501, too, film stars and politicians and European playboy princes. Meggie waved at them from the stage.

"Then you will be the first among your friends to report back about a speakeasy, Mummy," Lulu said. "You will be the center of attention at the next tennis club tea. Jessica's friend Margaret says it's really quite respectable here. Even the governor visits from time to time. And isn't that a Gish sister?"

Lady Hatton gave another sniff. "Margaret. She has always been a terrible influence, even when you were at school."

"But she is finding good stage roles here," Jessica said. "Everyone raves about her voice. She's sure to be cast in a Broadway show soon."

"A lord's daughter on the stage!" Lady Hatton gasped. She was only silenced when the handsome maître d' appeared to show them to a table on the mezzanine.

Jessica lingered behind to wave back at Meggie. Meggie winked, sparkling all in silver in the spotlight. She'd told Jessica they absolutely *had* to come to the d'Or, but she hadn't said why. Jessica half-hoped for another story idea, another interview for her growing collection. Maybe even a lead to someone who knew where to find Frank or his aunt. She hadn't seen a trace of him in days and couldn't think about anything else. Was he okay? Did he ever think of her, too?

"Jessica!" her mother called.

She turned to follow them up the stairs and suddenly found she couldn't move at all. Her brocade shoes seemed to be glued to the parquet floor. Standing right there in front of her, as if he had been conjured up in her thoughts like a genie, was Frank Markov.

He looked even more handsome than ever, his dark hair brushed back from the stark, elegant angles of his face, his dark evening jacket perfectly tailored to his lean body. He smiled at her, and she felt the fluttering mix of relief, joy, and anger deep inside of her.

"Where have you been?" she blurted out and almost clapped her hand over her mouth. Was that all she could say? After all the times she had envisioned their next meeting, all the sophisticated, blasé things she planned to say? She felt her cheeks turn warm with a blush and was glad it was dimly lit in there.

"My behavior has been unforgivable, I know," he said, his accent strong, his voice low and rough. "That is why I asked your friend Lady Margaret to bring you here tonight. I feared if I invited you myself you wouldn't come. Or if I came to your flat you would slam the door in my face."

"*You* had Meggie ask me here?" Jessica glanced over at her friend. Meggie just shrugged and smiled, mouthing the word *surprise*. "But why? How?"

"I am managing this place, of course. It is my new Club 501, for a time," Frank answered.

"So you don't work for the police anymore?" She wanted to clap her hand over her mouth again.

Frank laughed. "I do, but you may not want to say that quite so loudly. There is still the mystery of that poor young lady in the alley to decipher and many people in the city who would harm innocent citizens again."

So he was still an undercover bootlegger, trying to right the wrongs of the world. A grudging admiration pushed aside the anger that still lingered, and she gave him a reluctant smile. "So you're still the gallant soldier."

"Just a man trying to get by in a new world," he said. "I hear you, too, have a new job."

"So I do. Still writing at the *World* for now, but no more garden parties. You read my first story?"

"I did," he said, still smiling. "And I want very much to talk to you about it. But right now, that isn't why I wanted to see you tonight."

"It wasn't?" Jessica said. She could hardly breathe from wondering what he *did* want, from just being close to him again.

"Jessica! Come here this minute. Who is that you are talking to now?"

Jessica glanced up to see her mother glaring down at them from her table at the edge of the mezzanine. Jessica ached to know what Frank was going to say. Every nerve end seemed to hum just from him standing there, from the suspense of wondering what would happen next. But she knew her mother wouldn't rest until she was satisfied.

"Come," Jessica said. She tentatively reached out to take his arm, and she felt the tension of his muscles beneath her touch, the slight tremble of him. Good—so he wasn't so completely unaffected, either. "You should meet my mother."

"Your mother?" he said, his expression flashing into alarm.

Despite everything, Jessica had to laugh. "Come on. She's surely nothing to worry about after the Tsar of Russia."

She led him up the stairs to the table where her mother and Lulu waited. Lulu was smiling brightly while their mother glared like a gorgon in a mint-green satin turban.

"Mama, Lulu, may I introduce the Prince Romanov-Markov? He is a cousin to the late tsar," Jessica said mischievously. "Prince, this is my mother, the Countess Hatton, and my sister, Lady Louisa Carlisle." She had to admit she took a certain satisfaction in the new expression that came over her mother's face, an indulgent smile sweeping away the fierce frown.

"Lady Hatton, Lady Louisa, how charming to meet you at last," Frank said with an elegant smile, bowing over their hands with perfect Slavic manners. "I see where Lady Jessica gets her beauty. I hope you are enjoying your time in New York. It will surely not be the same after you leave."

"Well, I must say I should not have worried so very much about Jessica if I had known what fine gentlemen were here in this wild city," Lady Hatton said with a flutter of her feathered fan. "How shocking you must find her after the ladies of your own country! Why, I once heard Queen Alexandra herself remark on the great refinement of the poor young grand duchesses."

"Lady Jessica has been the very image of charm and grace, Lady Hatton, and a great credit to her family, I do assure you," Frank said soothingly. "It has been such a comfort to me here, so far from my home, to know her. Which is why I must beg now for permission to dance with her."

"Of course," Lady Hatton said. She was distracted by the waiter setting up an ice bucket for a bottle of champagne next to the table as Lulu giggled.

Jessica took Frank's arm as he led her onto the crowded dance floor. It was a waltz, even slower than usual because of the large crowd, intimate and lovely.

"Thanks for that," Jessica said, still stunned by the ease with which he had dealt with her mother. "She won't nag me so much about 'the company I keep' in New York now."

"Your mother and sister are lovely, just like you," Frank said with a laugh. His cool breath stirred the short strands of hair at her temple, making her shiver. "Will you go back to England with them now?"

Jessica shook her head. "Not for a while, though I know I'll have to eventually." She could see the importance of family now, the importance of love and loyalty, partially thanks to Frank and his aunt and seeing all they had lost. "I've agreed to move to a better flat, though, and they've agreed to let me stay until I finish my new job."

"Your new stories, you mean?"

"Yes. My editor loved the one I did about Russian émigrés, and it made the donations to charities for refugees increase. I want to keep doing that, if I can. I want to help."

"And I know you can. The words in your story had great power, Jessica, great humanity. You have such a gift." His arms tightened around her. "And you have made me see the hope in the world again, which I had thought was vanished. You make me want to do good again, too."

They suddenly went still in the middle of the dance floor. Other couples bumped into them, but Jessica barely noticed. Frank's arms were so close around her, his wonderful words echoing in her mind, and that was all she knew. The warmth of him, the spicy scent of his cologne, the bright blue of his eyes as he looked down at her.

"I'm glad you're staying in New York, Jessica," he said.

She smiled up at him. "I'm glad you're staying, too. More than I can say."

Something flickered in his eyes, and his smile faded. "I know I have no right to ask this, not after everything that's happened," he said. "But could I perhaps take you to dinner? Somewhere proper, of course. No speakeasies."

Jessica laughed, startled and delighted by his words. "Why, Prince. Are you asking me on a *date*?"

He grinned down at her, and it was like the sun suddenly came out in the world again. "Is that what they are calling courtship now, Lady Jessica? Very well. Will you go on a date with me?"

Jessica leaned her cheek against his chest and smiled. She could feel the fine wool of his coat on her skin, could hear the steady, strong beat of his heart. In that moment, she saw all that had happened to them, the dancing, the kiss, the raid, and all that could happen to them soon. Together.

A date. Imagine that.

"Dinner," she whispered, "might just be a good place to start."

Martini Club 4: The 1940s

Perilous

Prologue

Martha's Vineyard, late summer 1939

How much she hated the end of things.

Madeline Carlisle sat on the blanket spread over the soft, crumbly sand of the beach with her four best friends, watching the waves break and sweep away again, just as they had hundreds of times before. Every summer of their fourteen years, even from when they were babies who couldn't even crawl, they had sat on blankets just at this very spot, within view of their parents' cottages, picnic baskets and books and parasols spread then just like now.

It was Maddie's favorite place in the world, a place so very different from the rain and ancient history of her parents' English manor house, her school in Devon. Martha's Vineyard was all sun and sand, the smell of coconut oil, the taste of lobster and lemonade and rock candy. The laughter of her friends.

They had only really become her best friends because her Aunt Jessica and Uncle Frank hadn't any children of their own, so every summer Aunt Jess "borrowed" her and brought her to their cottage to visit *her* best friends. Their daughters, all the same age as Maddie, were like the sisters she didn't have in England. She lived all year for her summers with them.

And *this* summer had been just as glorious as all

the others. Bike rides into town to buy ice cream and movie magazines, swimming in the ocean, games of charades at night, whispered confidences on the back porch when they were supposed to be asleep.

Yet now the light had started to change, as it always did when August started to slip into September and the island grew quieter, houses shut up and businesses closing for the season. The sunsets were earlier every evening, the breeze off the ocean carrying a new chill. It meant summer was almost over. She would go back to England, to her parents and school, and the others would scatter as well. Iris to Philadelphia, Sophie to her own school in New York, Audra to wherever her singing star mother was performing.

There would always be letters, of course, flying back and forth over the Atlantic, sharing every detail of their lives even when they couldn't be together. And the months would slip by, Christmas, school exams, until she boarded a ship with Aunt Jess again. Summer, and her friends, would always come back.

Today felt different, though—different from all those other partings. Their parents thought the girls didn't know what was going on, that they were too young and giddy to know what was really happening in the world. No one could escape the truth, though, not much longer. It loomed over the summer beach like a dark cloud or a zeppelin, gathering momentum with every second.

Uncle Leo, Iris's father, listened to the wireless at night, and Maddie and the others would huddle in the shadows at the top of the stairs to eavesdrop. Hitler's German army was growing, his speeches growing bolder. He intended to take over all of Europe and would run over anyone in his way. It was just like the last war, barely twenty years ago, the one where Maddie's father got his scars and the nightmares that still made him shout in the night sometimes.

There was no telling what would be happening in the world next summer. Or when Maddie would see her friends again.

She stretched her legs out in front of her and dug her toes deep into the warm sand. Her skin was tanned a pale gold below the hem of her white shorts, and the afternoon had been so warm the strands of her cropped black hair stuck to the back of her neck. A cooler breeze blew now, though making her shiver.

She studied her friends, Iris, Audra, and Sophie. Sophie, as always, had her head bent over her sketchbook, her brown hair falling forward as her pencil flew. Audra was telling Iris some wild story about one of her mother's tours, and Iris was giggling, which was a good thing since she was usually so serious. They were all so very different, prankster Sophie, determined Audra, sweet Iris. No one seeing them would believe they were sisters, but they certainly were, deep in their hearts.

"It's almost that time, girls," she said.

"Oh, no!" Audra cried. "How can it be?"

"She's right," Iris said in her quiet, steady way. "We'll all have to leave next week. Our mothers will probably keep us busy packing until then."

"Not *my* mother," Audra muttered. "She's already gone to her newest show, all the way in San Francisco."

"You're lucky," Sophie said, not glancing up from her sketchbook. "*My* mother is always looking over my shoulder, like a worried old hen. I can't imagine why."

Maddie laughed. She certainly knew why Sophie's mum hovered like that. Out of all of them, Soph was by far the most likely of them to get into mischief. Her pranks were legendary on the island.

"The point is," Iris said, "we might not have another afternoon alone after this. We have to declare it now."

"Yes," Maddie said. Every year, at the end of the summer, the four of them would declare their greatest hopes for the future. Their wishes had changed over the years, but some things stayed the same. "Iris, you first."

Iris closed her eyes tightly, as if blowing out a birthday candle for a wish. "I want to go to medical school, to be a doctor. Or at least a nurse."

"You would be wonderful at that," Audra said, and indeed Iris would. She had a deep concern for people, a real desire to be of help wherever she could.

Iris shook her head. "Mom would never let me. She talks all the time about who I might marry in society, the security a husband with a grand Main Line house would give me. And Dad always sides with her. For a man who runs the best boxing gym in Philadelphia, he's just a softie when it comes to Mom. It doesn't matter how well I do in school she'll never see I won't make the same mistakes she did. But I can still hope."

"I declare I will never be like *my* mother, either," Audra said. They seldom saw Audra's glamorous mother Meggie on Martha's Vineyard, she was so busy with her career. When she did appear, it was like magic fairy dust had been sprinkled over the island. "I want to help other people, too, not just think of myself all the time. Being famous, getting people to applaud me—it's all so phony. Maybe I'll be a social worker."

"It's not *just* phony, you know," Sophie said, her pencil still flying over her sketchbook. She blew out a breath to push back a strand of hair from her eyes.

Audra frowned at her. "What do you mean?"

"Aunt Meggie makes people happy, too, in her own way," Sophie said. "It's been such a dismal decade, so many people struggling and unhappy, and her songs make them smile a bit. That's important."

Audra lay back on the blanket, still looking doubtful. "Well, then, what do *you* want to do with your life, Soph?"

"Paint, of course!" Sophie declared. "Make pictures so beautiful people will crowd around them in galleries, awestruck at my genius. Just like those Degas we saw at the Met last month. Remember, Maddie?"

Of course Maddie remembered. The four of them had been taken for the weekend to the city by Iris's mother to see a show and get some new dresses. She took them to the museum, and Maddie and Sophie had been so enraptured by a small room filled with Degas paintings and drawings that the guards had to chase them away at closing time. The movement and color of them were amazing. "They were incredible."

"And my work will surpass them!" Sophie dropped her sketchbook and took off in a flying jete across the sand in her polka dotted swimsuit, her slim, small body lithe and brown from the sun. "See, I'm a Degas dancer now!"

Maddie laughed and jumped up to join her in the dance. They clasped hands and twirled and leaped until Audra and even dignified Iris joined them. They spun around, splashing in the waves.

They fell, breathless with laughter, back onto the blanket. Lying in a circle, holding hands, they watched the sky slowly darken over their heads. The joy of the dance slipped away like a silk scarf between their hands, leaving only uncertain night.

"What about you, Maddie?" Audra asked. "What will you do?"

Maddie thought about it. Like Sophie, she loved art, loved the way its beauty transcended the scariness and pain of the human world, but unlike Soph she had no ability to create it herself. Maybe she could guide other people to see its meaning, though, teach them to see what she saw there.

"I suppose I'll try to go to university," she said. "My father has a cousin who is a don at Lady Matilda College at Oxford. If I could get a place there, I could take a degree in art history."

"You would make the most marvelous English bluestocking, Maddie," Audra said.

"And maybe help me get into some good London galleries," Sophie said teasingly.

"I wonder what our wishes will be the next time we meet," said Iris.

They all fell silent, but Maddie knew they were all thinking, fearing, exactly the same thing. If and when war came, who knew if they would ever even meet again at all?

Chapter One

London — 1947

Maddie Carlisle sped on her bicycle through the crowded lanes of Piccadilly, away from the quiet of her parents' old Georgian townhouse and into the thick of the crowds headed to work at shops or offices or warehouses. They were like an army of men and women in gray and brown suits and tan mackintoshes, packed in close together but not talking, not looking at each other. Everyone intent on getting through their own days.

Even two years after the end of the war, London held onto the residue of grimness. Rationing was still in effect, no sweets to delight, not enough meat for a proper Sunday roast, no bright, pretty, new clothes or high-heeled shoes. Every day she cycled past empty lots filled with rubble, still not completely cleared away after the Blitz. There was too much rebuilding to do, and not enough young men left to do it. They said that Princess Elizabeth would get married later in the year, a happy event to look forward to, but that seemed like a fairytale.

She turned toward Hyde Park. It was the long way 'round to her work, but she needed a bit of the relief of moving that morning.

She hadn't been in London for most of the worst of the war. She'd been at her boarding school, and then at

Oxford, her parents forbidding her to come into the city very often. But her father, Sir David Carlisle, who had been gravely wounded in the Great War, had been made an honorary colonel and worked long hours at Churchill's underground war rooms, creating military strategies according to coded messages. Her mother, Lulu, and Aunt Jessica worked at canteens and organized homes for war orphans, among other things.

School had seemed so unimportant against what was happening in England and to the rest of the world. Now that she was grown-up, she could see there was still much work to be done, and she could be a part of it.

She pedaled through the main gates into the park, and it was like entering a whole new world. It was a beautiful spring day, warm and soft, the worst of the winter banished. The sky opening up beyond the old chimneys and towers of rubble was a breathtaking bright blue. Flowers bloomed tentatively in their beds beside the gravel paths, little pops of hopeful red, yellow, purple. A few nursemaids in crisp gray uniforms pushed prams there, and dogs pranced along on their leads. A pair of lovers embraced on one of the benches, and old men played at skittles. Just like before the war.

But that world was gone. *Keep Calm And Carry On* the signs said for all those nightmare years, and everyone had done it. They had joked about the air raid sirens, the bad tea served in the shelters. After the war, they said, it will be normal again. Yet it wasn't; it couldn't be. The ugliness of the world had cracked open in all its horror, and it couldn't be put together again. Though they could all try.

Maddie pedaled faster, the wind catching at the curls of her black hair tucked up under the edge of her hat. The sun felt delicious, bathing her in its warmth, and she thought of Martha's Vineyard. The beach, the sand, and the waves—the laughter of her friends. It all seemed so far away now.

She emerged from the park onto the tony streets around Kensington Palace. Before the war, the neighborhood had been a place of luxury shopping, discreet storefronts with small brass plaques announcing couturiers, milliners, furriers, and jewelers, patronized by the Queen and the Duchess of Kent and their sets. It hadn't sustained any direct hits during the Blitz, but the buildings had been mostly shut up, the owners fled to the countryside. Now, it was slowly coming back to life, doors opening again, windows displaying ribbons and ruffles and feathers. A woman emerged from one shop, her gray suit and plain brown hat almost shabby-looking. Yes, despite the almost decrepit old hat, Maddie knew it was the Duchess of Portland.

Maddie found her way to a tall, narrow building at the end of the row, gleaming with a new white coat of paint. The sign on the glossy black door read, *Monsieur P. Gilles, Fine Art and Antiques.*

She rode around to the narrow lane behind the shops and left her bike there at the mews. She was running late, and the knowledge made her heart pound as she ran up the back stairs. This job meant so much to her, and it had only been hers for a few weeks after a short trial period. She couldn't afford to make a mistake.

In the dimly lit back corridor, she unpinned her hat

and tried to tidy her hair into its French chignon, which had seemed so elegant when she left the house. At school, she had just tied its thick length back into a braid, but that would no longer do. She was a lady now, with a proper job, and she had to look like it. But the hair, like the smart gray suit which had once been her mother's, still felt like a sham, a costume.

"Miss Carlisle? Is that you?" she heard Monsieur Gilles call.

"Yes, monsieur, it's me," she answered and hurried down the corridor. The back of the building was all shabby carpets and peeling wallpaper, a twisting warren of storage rooms. Once through the doorway, though, it was a new world.

Monsieur Gilles had once owned one of the finest art galleries in Paris, and before that in St. Petersburg, catering to royalty and aristocracy and a few American Gilded Age millionaires wanting to buy some taste. Maddie's Uncle Frank, Aunt Jess's absurdly handsome husband, had once been a Russian prince before he was run out of his home by the Revolution, and he had helped Monsieur Gilles escape. Then the old man escaped again, one step ahead of the Nazis, from Paris.

Now he was establishing his work in London and had agreed to hire Maddie, with the ink barely dry on her Art History degree, as a junior assistant.

Her breath caught a bit, as it always did, when she stepped into the gallery itself. It was so simple yet so elegant, with ice-blue walls trimmed in antique white plasterwork, an Aubusson rug of pale pink roses and blue ribbons on the parquet floor, gilded French chairs upholstered in blue brocade gathered around an easel where special works could be displayed. Art hung on the walls, discreetly lit to call attention to their perfections—Monets, Renoirs, an old Master or two, Gainsborough portraits, Fantin-Latour flowers.

Monsieur Gilles sat at his marble and gilt Louis XV desk at the far corner of the room, his gray head bent over an open catalog, his magnifying glass in hand. He himself was, as always, impeccably dressed in a well-cut dark suit and pastel tie, a small pink carnation in his buttonhole, but the desk was piled untidily high with art books and catalogs bristling with place markers.

"I'm sorry I'm late, monsieur," Maddie said, hurrying across the room to his side. The low heels of her gray suede court shoes, also borrowed from her mother, clicked on the polished floor.

"Not at all, *ma chere*," he answered in a distracted manner. "It's a slow morning. You are getting ready for your journey, *n'est-ce-pas?*"

"Of course. I'm off to America in a fortnight for my friend's graduation from Roseline. She's getting her degree in Art." Maddie felt her excitement return just to say the words—going to America! She hadn't seen her friends since before the war, and she ached to know how they were.

"She must send me some of her work, then. I am always hoping to find the next great new talent before anyone else." He held out the magnifying glass. "Look at these, mademoiselle. I know how you love Degas. What do you think?"

Curious, and cautiously excited, Maddie took the glass. So far, her work at the gallery consisted of unpacking crates and checking inventory, serving customers tea or pouring champagne, but she also tried hard to learn all she could about the art around her.

She gazed down at the open catalog. It wasn't like any other she had ever seen, columns of photos, some of them quite blurry, of paintings hanging on walls or propped up on floors. Most appeared to be in museums or galleries, but a few were obviously in drawing rooms or bedchambers. What little text was there was in French, and she had to translate quickly in her mind.

"What is this, monsieur?" she asked. "A new auction?"

Monsieur Gilles sighed. His face, so thin behind his well-groomed gray beard, so heavily lined with all he had seen, looked even sadder than usual. "Alas, *non,* mademoiselle. I have been asked by some of my friends in Paris and Vienna to assist in their efforts to recover some works that vanished in the war."

Maddie shivered. "Looted, you mean? Hidden by the Nazis?"

Monsieur Gilles rubbed at his eyes. "They hope to recover them for the rightful owners or their heirs, if such a thing is even possible. It seems a Sisyphean task."

"I know much was found in the mines at Altaussee in Austria," she said. "Even the Ghent Altarpiece. I am sure these are also out there somewhere."

"Indeed. There was a lady, a very brave lady, who worked at the Louvre during the war, a certain Madame Vallon. She was able to keep records of many Nazi shipments, and those records have already found a few important pieces. She and others are compiling books of images to send out to dealers so we can see if they come through our galleries."

Maddie studied the photos again, especially one of

a Klimt portrait that obviously hung in a lady's luxurious bedroom. She flicked through the pages and recognized styles but no specific paintings. "I don't remember any of these, monsieur."

"Nor do I, sadly. Perhaps you recall Madame Fortin, who visits the gallery often?"

"Of course." In the short time Maddie had been working there, she had seen Madame Fortin, an elegant lady of middle age who wore beautiful furs and feathered hats, several times.

"Her maiden name was Rosenberg, her grandfather a collector of great note in Salzburg. Except for what she brought with her to France on her marriage, the collection has vanished, and she wants to find as much of it as she can. The poor lady. One of Monsieur Rosenberg's favorite paintings was a Degas. Two dancers on stage, others watching from the wings, a bit on the large size for his usual work but still quite portable." He tapped at the page. "Your eyes are younger than mine, mademoiselle. What do you see there?"

Maddie used the glass to examine the photo. It was a line of paintings propped up against a bare wall, two Nazi soldiers studying them. She recognized a Berthe Morisot of a lady in an elaborate hat on a balcony, a Renoir of children at the park, a couple of less-than-stellar landscapes. And at the end of the row...

Was it really? She leaned so close she bumped her head on the desk. The photo was gray, blurry, but she could see the gauzy tutus, the gracefully outflung arm of a dancer in mid-pirouette. She had a sudden vision of Sophie twirling on the beach. *I'm a Degas dancer now!*

She read the caption. "Schloss Ansburg, 12/43."

"Madame Fortin's Degas?" she said.

"Perhaps. It does match the description."

"Where did this lot of paintings go?"

"The Schloss Ansburg was a large clearing station in Austria, it was run by a man named Hans Emmerling of Munich." Monsieur Gilles's mouth twisted in a frown. "I met him once or twice before the war. He had a gallery of some repute back then, specializing in Impressionists. But he turned his artistic eye to the pay of the Nazis, like many others. I have a friend at the Metropolitan in New York, a Mr. Sanders, who has been on the trail of these for quite some time."

Maddie heard the deep, bitter sadness in his voice. "What happened to Emmerling? To the paintings he took?"

Monsieur Gilles shrugged. "He vanished. I hear whispers he went to South America, but who really knows? The Degas could be in Buenos Aires now. Or..."

Or destroyed, as so many other works had been.

Maddie remembered Sophie's letter, the one she had read just last night after she got home from work. Sophie's suspicions of her art professor. "Monsieur, I think maybe..."

The bell over the door sang out, breaking into her words. She turned to face the customer, grateful for the interruption. What could she have said, really, that wouldn't sound silly? An art student friend with vague suspicions of forgeries? Maddie knew she couldn't say anything else until she had learned more, and that would have to wait until she could talk to Sophie in person.

It was Lady Ives who stood there, swathed in furs,

her little dog in her arms. "Monsieur! I heard you have the loveliest little Louis XVI clock, I must see it."

Monsieur's tired, gray expression vanished into a charming smile, and he hurried to take Lady Ives's gloved hand in his to bow over it. "Indeed I do, it would be perfection in your drawing room. Perhaps you would care for a small glass of champagne first? A little peek at some Boucher drawings? I thought only of you the minute I saw them."

Maddie hurried away to pour out the champagne, and she didn't have a moment to stop after that. It was a busy day of work, with a few new shipments arriving that had to be cataloged and two paintings packed to be sent to their new homes in Edinburgh and Brighton. But as Maddie rode her bicycle away from the gallery in the evening, her body was exhausted even as her mind still raced over the lost Degas.

Instead of turning toward home, she rode on to Trafalgar Square. It was a nice evening, starting to turn to springtime warmth, and crowds were gathered around the lions, laughing and singing in the sunset. It was still wondrous, the freedom to wander the city at night unafraid of air-raid sirens.

At a kiosk outside the National Gallery, she found just what she was looking for, a postcard of Degas's *Ballet Class*. She borrowed a pencil from the man behind the counter. *Have an intriguing mystery on the go—desperately need your help. Remember the Degas!* She scribbled on the back and addressed it to Sophie in her dormitory at Roseline. Hopefully it would get there before Maddie did.

Chapter Two

Vienna
"Wenn ich sonntags in mein Kino geh..."

The singer was scarcely the finest the rundown, shabby Club Bleu had heard in many years, but she was a tall, willowy blonde with a low, smoky voice, dressed in a slinky black silk dress, and that was all that was required. Her eyes were closed, and she swayed a bit in the murky spotlight as she sang the old song from the 1930s, making the cheap fabric of her dress shimmer and drawing the rapt attention of everyone in the room. She was good, as Christoph Von Albrecht well knew. His organization had placed her there for that very reason.

Christoph sat back in his chair in the corner of the room, taking a drag on his expensive American-bought cigarette and exhaling a silvery plume as he examined the crowd. Before the war, Club Bleu was one of the most exclusive in Vienna. Aristocrats, movie stars, artists, they all went there. Even during the war it didn't quite go out of style, for the Nazi Emmerling and his officers liked going there to drink champagne brought from Paris and meet the charming girls. Now, it was faded, the gilt trim on the walls flaked away, the velvet curtains threadbare.

Bleu's best days were behind her, just like Vienna itself. The world of Christoph's boyhood, the world his parents inhabited of sophistication and art, would never come back, not entirely. But many people, like himself, were working in secret to regain just a little of the glory their city had once been.

His contact was late, yet that was nothing unusual. An Austrian's acute sense of punctuality was not everyone's, and since the man was a wonder at ferreting out secrets from every back street he deserved a bit of consideration. Not too much more, though. Christoph glanced at his watch. He didn't want to spend too much more time at Bleu, he had other places to be that night, other meetings to make.

"More schnapps, mein herr?" he heard a soft voice say and glanced up to see one of the cocktail servers standing by his small table. At first glance, she could have been any girl he knew in his youth, with rounded pink cheeks, blonde braids pinned in a coronet atop her head, a dirndl skirt and ruffled blouse. But a closer look showed the wariness in her blue eyes, the hard lines around her mouth, the way her printed skirt was hemmed much shorter than a true dirndl should be.

She made him think of how many young lives had been destroyed in the war, including his own, spent hiding and fighting and hating. He had wanted to study art as a boy, to bring beauty into the world. How foolish that seemed now.

"A bit more, danke, fraulein," he answered.

She smiled and leaned closer, so close the loose neckline of her lacy blouse gaped. "Are you sure that will be all? Our rates are very reasonable here at Bleu."

He gave her a gentle smile. "Only schnapps tonight, I think."

Her lips pursed in disappointment, and she spun

away in search of more lucrative custom. Christoph caught the gaze of the singer. She tilted her head infinitesimally and nodded. Christoph followed her stare to find that his meeting had arrived at last. The man he knew as Oskar lingered there at the entrance for a moment, his plain brown hair and shabby brown tweed coat blending into the background.

The singer winked, and Christoph knew that meant no one suspicious lingered in the crowd at the moment. He waved Oskar over to the table. The man shambled over and dropped into the seat opposite Christoph and drained his glass of schnapps.

"Any word from Bremerhaven?" Christoph asked. Their organization's latest quarry, after the last two had been tracked, captured, and imprisoned, their art treasures redeemed, was a man named Emmerling, once an art dealer in Munich who came to Austria as a gaulieter after the Anschluss. His position of power and knowledge of art meant he could commandeer trainloads of the finest masterpieces to be sent to his estate back in Germany. His wife had been apprehended when the Americans moved into Austria, and with her a large shipment of Impressionists, but Emmerling himself had vanished. The walls of his mansion were stripped bare, and his greatest stolen work, a Degas of two dancers on a stage, gone.

But the world was a smaller place than villains like Emmerling seemed to think, and they couldn't run forever. Emmerling had been traced to Bremerhaven, where he would have to find passage on a ship bound for some distant port.

"He was there, under the name Peter Kurth, but there was a positive identification of him as

Emmerling," the other man answered after he downed another drink. The pretty waitress brought more, putting it down silently in front of him and then vanishing. The man took out a small packet of papers from his coat pocket and slid it over to Christoph. "He took out these shipping manifests for four large crates. He himself did not travel with them. He was tracked onto a smaller ship bound for South America and has been followed there. No word yet on his current whereabouts."

Christoph scanned the papers, four crates filled with "family paintings," listed of little worth. "New York?" Nazis fleeing with their spoils often divided up their shipments, hoping to baffle anyone who might follow them, and then would claim them later. Or they might be bound for buyers or galleries who would not ask too many questions to obtain something like a Degas.

"The dockworkers we bribed confirmed the crates did contain paintings, but they couldn't say what exactly. These were the descriptions we got." He handed over another paper.

Christoph read of landscapes, a still-life or two, a portrait of a mother and child—and some dancers on a stage, others watching from the wings. "It definitely sounds like the Goldstein Galerie collection." The Goldstein Galerie had been a very important salon before the war, selling pieces to important Jewish collectors like the Bloch-Bauers, until they fled before the war, leaving behind a large inventory. It had been one of the first places Emmerling visited when he arrived in Vienna.

"What will you do now?"

Christoph smiled. "Head for New York, of course, before the trail goes too cold. Who knows what we might find there in the end..."

Chapter Three

THE SOUTH END SLAYER STRIKES AGAIN!

The bold, black headlines seemed to scream out from the newspapers, taking up half the front page. Maddie opened it out on the small table in front of her seat and read in growing horror as the train sped on its way from New York to Boston. It sounded like a Jack the Ripper type killer was running loose in the South End, killing any vulnerable women he could find alone.

She remembered Iris writing that she and Audra were doing some work at a soup kitchen in just that area, and Maddie shivered to imagine her friends walking there alone at night. Footsteps behind them in some alley, the two of them walking faster in fear, then running...

"Stop it," Maddie whispered to herself. Her friends knew how to take care of themselves; she knew she shouldn't worry about them at all. But their hearts were so kind they would never give up helping someone, even if they put themselves into danger. She couldn't wait to be with them again, to see for herself they were safe and hear what had really been happening in Boston lately.

It had all been much too long since they were together, whole lifetimes seemed to have passed between with them with the never-ending war. She had felt so alone an ocean away from them. Would they even be the same friends she remembered now?

She turned the page and read an article about the upcoming graduation season for all the prestigious universities. Harvard and Yale and Smith were all planning grand ceremonies, with parties galore to send a new crop of elite young graduates into the world. Maddie saw balls and garden parties listed, along with cocktail parties, plays and recitations, dinner and breakfasts.

At the bottom was a notice of an art exhibit at the Morwen Gallery for all the graduating Art majors, and Sophie's name was one particularly mentioned. *We expect to see the talented Miss Noble's work in New York and Paris by the end of the year!* Maddie quite agreed. Sophie had always been a brilliant mimic, able to copy any artist's style in any medium, as well as a hilarious caricaturist, but there was so much more to her talent than that. Since getting her own degree and working with Monsieur Gilles, Maddie could see that even more. Sophie had a real shot at a future in the art world.

But Maddie worried about her, too. Sophie was sometimes *too* talented, too independent. She carefully refolded the newspaper and tucked it under her stack of books.

"Can I get you some more tea, miss?"

Startled out of her daydreams, Maddie glanced up to see the train portress standing beside her with a refreshment trolley.

"Oh, yes, thank you. Tea and one of those sandwiches would be lovely," Maddie answered. "I'm meant to have lunch with my friends as soon as we arrive in Boston, but I'm already quite famished."

The lady poured out the tea with a smile. "You do have the prettiest accent, miss. Just like Greer Garson. You're English too, like her?"

"I am. I just traveled from London."

"You won't like *this* too much, I'm afraid. In the movies, the English seem so particular about their tea." She put down the cup and found a large ham sandwich to go with it.

Maddie laughed to look at the dark, murky brew in her cup. "Maybe not, but I *will* like the sandwich. Real ham, so heavenly." She laid out the paper to use as a tablecloth for the refreshments, unfolding it to the headlines again.

The portress frowned. "Terrible business, that."

Maddie glanced down at the paper, becoming frightened for her friends all over again. "Indeed. Have the police any leads at all yet?"

"Not yet, at least not anything they're saying. My sister works near there. I've been so nervous for her."

"I'm sure it must be terrifying."

The girl nodded and continued on her way with the cart. Maddie glanced up over the edge of her white china cup to find a man studying her. She had noticed him before, of course. The car was only half full, and he would be hard to miss in any case. The portress thought she sounded like a movie star, but this man definitely looked like he belonged on the screen. Tall, lean, and elegant in a well-cut gray suit, his hair a sunny gold, waving back from a face that was all cut-glass angles, with bright blue eyes. Definitely a matinee idol.

He gave her a small nod and smile, and Maddie felt her cheeks turning embarrassingly warm. Before she could get too flustered, he turned away to look out his window again.

She turned away herself to watch the passing scenery out her window. It was turning from farm fields and small villages to the outskirts of the city now, tall apartment buildings with washing flapping from the windows. Soon, they would pull into the elegant South Station, and her friends would be waiting. She was determined to put everything else—serial killers, art heists, and handsome, disconcerting strangers—out of her mind for the moment and just concentrate on that.

The train began to slow, sliding past tall office buildings and historic parks ringed with colonial buildings, until the station was finally in sight. They vanished into a tunnel, coming out in a covered, glass-like terminal, and jolted to a halt.

Maddie rose to her feet, smoothing the flared skirt of her new burgundy-red travel suit and making sure her hat was still on straight. She felt so nervous, so unsure, which was strange, considering she was about to see her oldest friends again. Maybe she feared they would be changed—or that they would think *she* was.

She reached up to fetch her carrying case from the overhead rack, but found she was too late. A gloved hand, an arm in an impeccably tailored gray wool sleeve, was already taking it down for her.

She glanced up to see it was the movie star, and he was even more handsome up close. His face looked like something in a painting, a Renaissance aristocrat with that starkly carved, perfect face and mesmerizing blue eyes.

"Thank you very much," she managed to say, grateful her voice didn't wobble. She felt so silly, like a flustered schoolgirl.

"My pleasure," he answered, his voice touched at the edges with a musical, Alpine accent.

He tipped his hat and gave her a small smile before he left the car. Maddie watched him go, somehow unable to look away from him. Could he possibly be German? What was he doing in Boston? Some sort of spy thing, maybe?

She suddenly realized she couldn't stand there all day making up wild stories about handsome, mysterious strangers. She had to find her friends.

She hurried down the train steps and onto the platform. At first she could see nothing through the sea of people rushing around her, everyone with important places to go or be.

"Maddie! Maddie, over here!" someone shouted. She spun around to find Sophie with Iris in in tow pushing their way through the crowd. Sophie was dressed as vividly as always in a red print skirt and blue sweater set, her hair flying from beneath her beret. Iris, as befitted her socially-aware mother, wore a fashionable but conservative pale cream suit and small hat.

And with that glimpse all Maddie's doubts vanished. They *were* still her friends, though older now just as she was. Their smiles were the same, their joyous welcome all she could have ever wished for. Maddie ran to them and found herself hugging all of them at once, laughing and crying at the same time, just as she was.

They talked over each other, their words tumbling out, tangled together. "How are..." "What are..." "Can you..."

"Oh, come on, we can't stay here! We can't hear

ourselves at all," Sophie said. "Let's go find some lunch, after we get your luggage of course. Audra is meeting us there. She had a quarrel with her mom." They all grimaced; Audra's arguments with Meggie were legendary.

"That sounds perfect," Iris agreed, her sweet calmness making them all slow down a bit.

Sophie grabbed one of Maddie's suitcases from the luggage department, and Iris linked arms with Maddie to lead her out of the station. "How was the journey?"

"Long and dreary, but quite uneventful," Maddie answered. "There weren't many other people on the ship, it wasn't like before the war at all."

"No handsome sailors to flirt with?" Sophie teased.

Maddie thought of the man on the train, with his golden beauty and mysterious accent. She decided not to mention him. "The crews still haven't recovered from the war, either. It's all old men on the passenger liners now."

"How gloomy!" Sophie cried. "Well, you're here now, and just wait until you see all the parties we have lined up."

"Uncle Harry says you have to come to the club tonight," Iris said.

"He has a special dance band lined up, just for you," Sophie said. "They're English, you see. It should be fun."

"Of course. I can't wait to see the place, we've heard so much about it," Maddie answered. "I feel like I haven't been to a proper nightclub in ages." Her attention was caught by the window of a bakery they were passing, a display of luscious-looking pastel cakes. "Or had a *real* cake. Sugar is still rationed, you know. I'm tasked with bringing back lots of chocolate for all my friends, and for Aunt Jess in particular."

"Mom can give you as much as you like," Sophie said. Her mother was one of the finest bakers in Boston. "She'll stuff you with so many sweets you'll never want another!"

"I doubt that could ever be true." Maddie suddenly glimpsed someone in the shop beyond the window, a flash of golden hair and gray suit. Could it be...it was! The man from the train, chatting and smiling with the lady behind the counter. She handed him a small envelope. "I haven't tasted a real cake since 1940."

"How absolutely horrid!" Sophie declared, tugging her away from the window. "Well, now you're going to have fun again. With the four of us together again, this town isn't going to know what hit it..."

****

Christoph noticed the woman as soon as she sat down in the half-empty train car in New York. Not because she was beautiful; she wasn't, not really, nor even particularly pretty, but she was quite striking. Very slim, with hair so dark it was almost black, pinned back in a French chignon, with winter-blue eyes and arching dark brows in a heart-shaped face. Her only makeup was a slightly unfashionable rose-pink lipstick.

It was a face that would have photographed well or looked stunning on film. At first he wondered if she was on her way to Hollywood with dreams of stardom, like so many others.

Yet she didn't seem the film-crazy type. She wore a burgundy and black suit, well-cut but a bit out of date in style, like the lipstick, and too mature for her age, with a matching plain burgundy felt hat. On her lapel was a small flower basket brooch, red and blue cabochon stones with emerald leaves in a pearl basket, with small pearls to match in her ears. So many girls had flower basket pins now, a trend Princess Elizabeth had started with a birthday present from her royal parents. Most of those were paste, of course, but Christoph's educated eye told him this brooch was real.

An English aristocrat, then, fleeing from gray London for a bit of fun? Why, then, did she look so solemn? He found himself intrigued by her story.

When she sat down, she took out a worn leather valise and brought out some newspapers, along with a thick stack of books. Christoph squinted to see the titles. *Harper's History of Art From Ancient Greece to 1900. The Impressionists: A Monograph.* Catalogs from Christies. When she spoke to the portress, she had a cut-glass English accent.

His interest was definitely piqued. An art student, then? Or perhaps something more? The English were searching for lost art treasures, too, and smugglers came in all shapes and forms.

It seemed most unlikely, of course, that a young lady connected with a Nazi smuggling scheme would happen to board the same train as him, yet he had seen such things happen before. Espionage could be so much clumsier than readers of thriller fiction thought.

Christoph watched her surreptitiously as the train gathered speed. She didn't do much, just read and sipped at her tea, sometimes looking out the window with a small frown on her face, as if worried about something. A couple of times, she glanced up and met his gaze, but then she would blush and look away quickly again. If she *was* a spy, she was a very good one. But he was inclined to think she was what she appeared, a well-bred young English lady, perhaps come to study art or work at an auction house before returning to London, to marry another aristocrat and help him run his tumbling-down stately home.

As the train slowed and pulled into the station, Christoph watched as she gathered up her books and newspapers, packing them away. The contemplative frowns were gone, replaced by nervous smiles. Maybe someone important was meeting her at the station? An exciting American to replace the dull English suitor. Christoph laughed at his fancies. He had no time for making up stories about pretty English girls, but he had enjoyed the small diversion. When he fetched her bag from the rack and told her "My pleasure," he certainly meant it.

When they stopped at the terminal, he took his time packing his own belongings, giving her space so she wouldn't think he was following her. But when he stepped into the crowd, tugging the brim of his hat low over his brow, he noticed her again at once. She stood in a knot with the other girls, all of them laughing and shrieking as young women always seemed to do when they met. Her face came alive when she laughed, her cheeks pink and glowing.

"Mr. Albrecht?"

Christoph turned to see a nondescript little man behind him, much like the agent who met him at Club Bleu, but much tidier in his dress and sober.

"Yes?" Christoph answered warily.

"I'm Mr. Perry, from the Art Institute. I was sent to take you to your hotel and to brief you on what has been happening with the Emmerling shipment. I'm afraid you'll have little time to rest, a meeting has been set for tonight at the Club 501."

"Thank you. The sooner I get started here the better. It's most vital that we act immediately before those works vanish like the others."

"Quite right." Perry led Christoph through the throngs of people, all of them meeting each other with tearful joy or quarrels or indifference, children dashing around people's feet, porters pushing their way through with carts of trunks. They took their place in line at the taxi stand. "I was in the US infantry unit in the war, one of the first to reach the mines at Altaussee," the man said. "I'll never forget it."

Christoph glanced at the man sharply. "Indeed? That must have been exciting. I was with a group of scholars trying to push our way through the Alps to help you evacuate those works but didn't make it. I spent months working on the cataloging of the works hidden at Neuchwanstein. Thousands of objects there, I thought we would never sort them all." He remembered it all so well. Classical statues, nineteenth century portraits, medieval illuminated manuscripts, jeweled tiaras, and heartbreaking piles of wedding rings, all jumbled together in the castle's drafty, unfinished halls. All of it stolen, almost lost forever.

"Then you remember what it was all like. Save and recover all you can. A minute of excitement, then months of paperwork."

Christoph laughed. "There is still excitement to be had in the salvation, I think."

"Let's hope so. People like Goering have taken enough." In the quiet of the taxi line, Perry frowned and said softly, "I think we may have a bit of a setback here."

"A setback?"

"An art professor at Roseline. We had him narrowed down as one of the people who was either covering up the stolen work with new stuff so it can leave the country without much scrutiny or just forging works outright. He was just a middleman between unscrupulous gallery owners and Herr Emmerling, but he could have told us a lot."

"Could have?"

Perry's lips pressed together in a grim line. "We can't quite find him. Evading us, you see. And his studio at the college was cleared out except for some student work he seemed to be grading."

"What of the students?" Christoph asked. "I remember my own university days, we copied all the time."

"We're looking into all that. None of them seem to have any German connections so far. They seem young to be Nazi collaborators."

Christoph stared blindly into the crowd. "Ah, but the Nazis loved the young. So impressionable, so easy to manipulate."

Perry gave him a sharp glance. "That's right. You're Austrian, aren't you, Mr. Albrecht?"

It was their turn for a taxi, and Christoph was silent as the backs were loaded and they got into the back seat, jolting ahead into the city itself. "Yes, I am Austrian, my father was a professor of literature in Vienna and collector of art in a small way," he answered as they drove past towering buildings and old colonial brick two-stories, jostling together. "When the Anschluss came, every Austrian family was told to send their sons to Hitler Youth meetings. That was when my father sent me to stay with my uncle in New York."

"And your parents?" Perry asked quietly.

Christoph shrugged. He had long ago learned to hide his real emotions when it came to his family. "Gone now, along with most of their own art collection. I have recovered a piece or two." The Degas drawings, the Holbein miniature of a lady of Henry VIII's court. Christoph carried that one with him everywhere to remind him of his family, his mission.

"That's tough," Perry said. "Maybe we'll find some of it here, though. You never know."

Christoph thought of the blue-eyed English girl, her laughing delight as she hugged her friends. "Anything is possible in this world. Now—tell me about this meeting tonight..."

Chapter Four

Maddie stepped into the elegant Park Plaza grill and paused for a moment to inhale the delicate scents of crab salad, baked bread as delicate white as a cloud, the expensive perfumes of the ladies (was that L'Heure Bleu?), fresh flowers in crystal vases, and the ineffable yet unmistakable crisp air of newness and luxury. It was all so familiar, from childhood visits with her "'aunts," and yet so very different from all those long, gray, drab years of war ad rationing and old clothes in England.

Even the colors seemed too vivid to be real, the blue and gold of the swagged and tasseled window draperies, the lush, flowered carpet under her feet, the gold satin cushions of the gilded chairs, the red and green and pinks of the ladies' dresses and suits, the feathers and flowers on their tilted hats atop curled hair.

"Are you all right, Maddie?" Iris asked, all gentle concern, as she had always been. Maybe Maddie *had* changed after the war, but her friends were still her friends. Her lovely, sweet sisters of the heart. "You suddenly look so sad."

Maddie gave her a bright smile. "How can I ever be sad, being here with all of you again? It's the loveliest day! It's just..."

"Just what?"

"How beautiful it all is. How bright and vivid and new. It's overwhelming."

161

"Of course it must be, after London. We heard it was so horrid," Iris said gently. "But that's all over now, and we're together again! And just wait until you taste the crab salad, you will love it."

Maddie laughed and linked her arm through Iris's. It was so like Iris to try to make everyone else happy when she must be worried herself about those awful stories of the South End Slayer. After all, Iris did so much charity work there.

"Come on, you two slow-pokes! They saved us our favorite table," Sophie called. She had hurried ahead, as usual, and stood next to a table next to one of the windows. She waved them over, practically bouncing on the toes of her fancy spectator pumps.

Iris and Maddie laughed and threaded their way past the tables of Molyneux-clad, Guerlain-scented ladies to their own table. A few of the matrons frowned to see that such *noisy* young ladies had claimed such a fine table, but Maddie didn't care. She wasn't working at the gallery today; she didn't have to worry about what such people thought for the moment. She didn't have to think about anyone else at all.

But she *did* think about the man on the train. His crooked smile. His beautiful eyes that saw too much. His hand on hers...

"Sit here, Maddie!" Sophie said, interrupting her thoughts of the handsome stranger with his musical accent.

"Ah, the Park Plaza," Maddie sighed as she sank into the soft, smooth satin seat, and traced her fingertips over the crisp white damask of the tablecloth. The silver gleamed, and the crystal sparkled, the lilies and roses in the Sevres vase sending their sweetness into the air. "It never changes."

Iris gave a wistful sigh as she took off her gloves. "If only everyone in the city was lucky enough to see it."

"If only." Sophie waved her hand, grinned her dimpled, irresistible smile, and champagne magically appeared them. "But *we* are lucky to be together again! How was your journey, Mads? Did you meet any dark, mysterious strangers like in *Dark Voyage*?"

Maddie remembered Christoph and his smile again. "Well, as a matter of fact..."

Sophie and Iris leaned forward avidly. "Yes?" they gasped together.

"There was someone on the train," Maddie whispered. "He helped me with my bag, asked about my books. He was quite good-looking, with such blue eyes..."

Sophie shook her head sadly. "I never have such luck on trains at all. I only meet the most unsuitable men."

Maddie was sure there was a tale in those words—Sophie's life was always filled with tales of delicious trouble—but there was no time to ask her about it at the moment. Sophie waved and called out, "Audra! Over here!"

Maddie turned to see Audra hurrying toward them, as gorgeous as always in a blue and white suit in the latest style, a large cartwheel hat tilted just so over her upswept hair. She screamed to see Maddie and ran forward to kiss her cheek, hugging everyone before she sat down and reached for her champagne glass. She gulped it down.

Even though she was as beautiful as ever, Maddie

feared she could see the remains of tears behind the makeup, a too-bright gleam in her friend's eyes.

"Oh, Audra, darling, what's wrong?" Iris asked gently. Sophie refilled Audra's glass.

Audra laughed and looked down to adjust her skirt. "Good heavens. What makes you think something is wrong?"

Iris touched Audra's gloved hand. "Did Uncle Harry..."

"No. It's—it's my mother," Audra blurted. "She waylaid me with tea and scones."

"But that's wonderful," Sophie said. "Things are better then?" She leaned close to Maddie and whispered, "Poor Audra and Aunt Meggie have been quarreling again; it's so sad."

"Oh, no," Maddie gasped. She dug a handkerchief out of her handbag and passed it to Audra, who dabbed at her eyes.

"I don't know what to think," Audra said.

"Can you enlighten us?" Maddie asked softly.

"My mother and Mr. Frisk, they're—I can't say it!" Audra wailed. "It's too awful."

"You mean—an affair?" Maddie said, stunned. Aunt Meggie was always busy, it was true, but she loved her family. Surely Audra was mistaken? Or had things truly changed so much over the years? *Oh, poor Audra*, she thought.

Sophie snorted and gestured for another bottle. "That is the most ridiculous notion you have ever uttered, Audra Faye. You cannot really believe they are..." She lowered her voice. "Leo is besotted, all right, but not with Aunt Meggie."

Maddie and Iris giggled, a little giddy with the

champagne and the thought of someone as old as Aunt Meggie having such a fling. With her agent!

Audra tossed them a baffled expression. "But I've never seen Leo with anyone at all. He—he *loves* my mother."

"Everyone loves your mother, Audra. She's Lady Margaret." Sophie picked up her leather-bound menu. "Now, I want to talk about my graduation party. It' on Friday, you know. And we still have not decided on our movie. I think something dark and thrilling, like *Boomerang*."

Everyone groaned. Sophie always picked the most depressing flicks.

"No murders," Iris said with a shudder. "Not with that dreadful South End Slayer in all the papers."

"Spencer Tracey and Katherine Hepburn are in *Sea of Grass*," Maddie suggested. They all liked Katherine Hepburn.

"I'm in," Iris and Audra chorused.

"Fine." Sophie sighed. "Now, shall we start with caviar? I think my father is paying the tab..."

Chapter Five

"Oh, it's gorgeous! Like something in a movie," Maddie exclaimed as they stepped into Uncle Harry's Club 501. "I expect Cary Grant and Irene Dunne to come dancing by."

"It *is* pretty swanky, isn't it?" Audra said. She couldn't quite hide the pride in her voice, even though she spent so much of her life trying to distance herself from her parents, to not be like them at all.

It was indeed swanky. It wasn't busy yet at barely nine o'clock, though the band was playing from their stage at one end of the room and a few couples circled the mirror-like dance floor. Maddie was able to study the club for a few minutes without a crowd in her way. The deep red velvet upholstery on the chairs and settees, the polished marble tables, the gleaming mirrors behind the bar, all breathed luxury and ease and comfort.

She caught a glimpse of herself in one of the mirrors and suddenly felt a bit awkward. She hadn't had a new evening dress in ages; silks and velvets were still hard to get on the rations, and her pre-war dresses were for a schoolgirl. She had borrowed one of her mother's gowns, and though Lulu was renowned in London for her chic fashion sense, the stark lines of white and silver satin didn't seem quite right for Maddie's figure. She tugged the draped neckline into place and smoothed the waves of her hair. At least diamond star hair clips never went out of style!

"Come on, slow-poke," Audra called, and Maddie was startled to see that her friend was already halfway to the bar. She hurried to follow her, skirting around the edge of the dance floor and past a cluster of tables of laughing parties. The bar was as elegant as the rest of the place, a long, polished expanse looking on back-lit shelves of jewel-bright liquors, emerald-green absinthe, ruby Campari, amber whiskey.

Just before they reached the bar, a tall, scrawny waiter with thinning hair bumped into them and then rushed away.

"Careful, Jim," Audra called. She gave Maddie a rueful smile. "That's Jim, a new waiter. Daddy says we have to let him have time to learn, but I'm not sure. Come on, let's get that drink."

"What'll it be tonight?" asked the burly, dark-haired bartender. He had a scarred face and narrowed eyes, and Maddie wondered if they had found him back in their parents' secret-shrouded Prohibition days in New York, when they gathered at Uncle Frank's Bungalow bar.

"Champagne, of course, Pauley," Audra said with a laugh. "Champagne is always the right thing, isn't it, Maddie?"

Maddie laughed. "I do like champagne, and I so seldom get any."

"Here you can have all you want, no ration books," Audra said. "Pauley, have you met Madeline? She's Aunt Jess's niece, her *real* niece, all the way from England. Maddie, this is the best bartender in Boston."

"I thought he must be," Maddie said. She took the

offered glass and savored the first sharp, yeasty taste of the bubbling liquid. It was just as wonderful as it should be, like drinking sunshine. "Nice to meet you, Pauley."

"And nice to meet you, Miss Madeline," he answered. "I learned everything I know about bartending from your Uncle Frank. Nice guy, even if he *is* a prince."

As Pauley turned away to serve another customer, a door in the corner opened, and Uncle Harry stepped out. His hair was going gray, but Maddie still had to say he was a very handsome man, tall and fit in his evening clothes, his eyes sparkling as he surveyed his little kingdom. "Lady Madeline!" he called in his deep, echoing voice, the voice Maddie remembered calling out for them in Martha's Vineyard evenings. It made her feel safe and comforted, just as it had then, and she couldn't object to his old name for her. Even though she *was* really just an Honorable. "So you're finally here. Maybe you can have a ladylike influence on Audra here. Wearing trousers all the time..."

"Oh, Uncle Harry, even Katherine Hepburn wears them in public now. Princess Margaret does the same. It's quite chic," Maddie answered with a laugh.

"So Audra keeps telling me," Harry grumbled.

Maddie kissed his cheek. "It is very good to see you again, Uncle Harry. I can't tell you how much I've missed you all."

A faint blush touched his creased cheeks. "Good to see you, too, kid. What are you drinking? Champagne? Pauley, make sure they have whatever they need. Dance, have some fun! Meggie should be here later, she'll be so happy you're here."

As Uncle Harry left to greet some new customers,

Maddie glimpsed Sophie stepping through the door, handing her wrap to the attendant to reveal a beautiful ruffled scarlet satin gown. Sophie was surrounded by a laughing crowd, as she usually was, sending them all into fits of giggles with her jokes. Maddie didn't recognize any of them, they were young men in evening jackets with their hair slicked back with too much brylcream and girls in stylish floral-print crepe gowns, their hems to the floor. She thought they must be Sophie's college friends. Art students, maybe? Perhaps one of them would know more about the stolen art.

Behind her was Iris, arm in arm with an aristocratic, hawk-faced young man dressed in the finest of New York-tailored tuxedos. Her fiancé? But Iris didn't look too happy about being with him as he whispered something in her ear, and they vanished into the crowd.

Maddie glimpsed someone slipping away from Sophie's crowd, disappearing into the noisy room. For a moment, Sophie seemed disconcerted, but she quickly recovered her usual grin.

"Maddie, darling, you're here already!" Sophie cried, pulling her attention from the swirling crowd. Sophie ran up and threw her arms around Maddie for a European double-kiss on the cheek. She smelled of her usual floral perfume with a hint of—was it gin? — underneath. Maddie pulled back to study her friend in concern. It wasn't like Sophie to pre-drink an evening out, she had enough *joie de vivre* with no alcohol at all.

"Are you quite all right, Soph?" she asked.

Sophie laughed, a too-bright sound. "Of course! How could I not be? It's always a fun night at 501."

Maddie leaned closer and whispered, "We have to

talk about the art. I need your help."

To her shock, she saw something like fear flicker across Sophie's face. Sophie glanced over her shoulder, as if trying to see who could overhear them.

"I know," Sophie whispered back. "But not here. Tomorrow? There are too many people here to talk quietly."

Maddie nodded, and two men came up to Sophie. They were handsome and laughing. But had obviously been drinking. Their cheeks were too flushed, their laughter too loud.

Sophie laughed, too, taking the men's arms. "Maddie, darling, these are two of the most hopeless flirts you could ever meet from Harvard, Bob and Geoffrey." She seemed like her usual merry self, yet there was an edge to her laughter now, something steely and desperate. "Gents, this is Madeline Carlisle, one of my very best friends. All the way from London."

"Pleased to meet you, Miss Carlisle," Bob, or maybe Geoffrey, said. "I'm afraid Sophie will give you the wrong idea about us!"

"We're the most gentlemanly gentlemen you could meet," Geoffrey, or Bob, said.

Maddie laughed. It was easy to get caught up in the happy-go-lucky atmosphere at 501; gray London seemed very far away. "Should I believe you?"

"Of course you shouldn't," Sophie said. "But they *are* heavenly dancers, I'll give them that."

"Let me prove it to you, Miss Carlisle," Bob or Geoffrey said. "May I have this dance?"

Maddie glanced at the dance floor. The band had just launched into a fox-trot, and the dancers glided and spun across the polished floor like a kaleidoscope.

"Thank you, Mr., er, Bob," she said, hoping she was right about his name. "I'd love to dance."

They spun onto the dance floor, and almost immediately she regretted it. He had definitely been pre-drinking and smelled like a whiskey still, his hands clammy through her dress as he held her too tightly. She glanced desperately over his shoulder at Sophie, who shrugged helplessly just before she vanished behind a wall of people.

"So you're from London?" he said as he clumsily twirled her, bumping them into another couple.

"I am, yes."

"Is it true what they say about English girls?"

"I don't know." Maddie gasped, trying to put some distance between them. "What do they say?"

He dragged her even closer. "That there's no men left in England, so you're all desperate for..."

"Please let me go," she said before he could go on. She pushed against his sweaty shoulders, feeling blocked in by the crowd. He just laughed and pulled her closer. She didn't want to make a scene in her uncle's club, but if she had to she would! What they had not told this cad about English girls was that they had learned to fight back. The Blitz hadn't been for nothing.

"I'm sorry, I do believe this is my dance," a deep, musically-accented voice said from behind Maddie as she and her partner bumped into another couple yet again. An arm, clad in a perfectly tailored black wool sleeve, slid between her and her unwanted partner and clasped her hand to twirl her away.

It all happened in an instant, as smoothly as something choreographed in one of those Cary Grant films. The young drunkard was left alone, sputtering helpless protests, pushed from the floor by the swirl of dancers. Maddie was spun back into the dance, led into the most elegant quickstep.

"Th-thank you," she gasped, breathless at how quickly the awkward moment was changed and saved, turned into something quite different. She glanced up at her tall rescuer's face and nearly stumbled again in surprise. She would certainly have fallen if not for his grasp on her hand and her waist.

It was the man from the train, the handsome, radiantly golden one. He smiled down at her, his sky-blue eyes sparkling as if he was highly amused by her predicament.

"Oh," she said. "I see you've helped me again."

His smile turned quizzical. "I beg your pardon?"

"On the train. You helped me with my suitcase."

"Ah, yes." His smile widened again, making adorable little creases at the edges of his eyes. He really was absurdly handsome, not like a real person at all. "I thought we might meet again."

He had noticed *her*? Maddie found herself feeling ridiculously pleased. "Really? In a city as big as Boston?"

"I had a feeling. My grandmother was a Romanian gypsy, you see, and passed down a great belief in fate."

A gypsy? Now Maddie was even more intrigued. What was his story? It had to be a doozy, she was sure. He didn't seem like anyone she had ever met before. He spun her easily around a corner and twirled her in a graceful arc. "At home, we couldn't even talk, let alone dance, without an introduction."

He laughed and spun her again. "But America is different. Isn't that what the Americans keep telling us?"

"That's true. I've been visiting America since I was a child, so I guess I can be an honorary one tonight." And she could be bold. She was among friends at Club 501, she was safe there. Except from her own infatuated feelings. But this was no callous, clumsy boy like Bob/Geoffrey. "I'm Madeline Carlisle."

His smile flickered. "You are related to Frank Markov, aren't you?"

Maddie was surprised. Was he a connection of Uncle Frank's, too? The man surely knew everyone, from exiled Russian duchesses to the guy who swept the street corner. "He's married to my Aunt Jessica. They don't have any children, so they've always sort of adopted me. How do you know him?"

"He helped a friend of mine, a Monsieur Gilles, to escape from a dangerous situation in the war."

There seemed no end to this man's surprises. "But I work for Monsieur Gilles! In his gallery in London. How extraordinary."

He gave her that eye-crinkling smile again, and she almost forgot everything else. She stumbled on her hem, but he rescued her with a smooth little lift. "You see, Miss Carlisle—I knew we were fated to meet."

"How do you know Monsieur Gilles? You certainly don't sound French."

"I was born in Vienna, but now I am a wanderer of the world." He twirled her around and back into his arms. "I am Christoph Albrecht, at your service."

Viennese? Maddie's suspicions rose up, coldly interrupting her romantic little champagne haze. What had he been doing during the war? Vienna had once been a center of cosmopolitan culture, music, and cuisine, and above all art. Art that had often vanished. "Why have you wandered now to Boston, Herr Albrecht?"

"For the art. I do a bit of dealing here and there, not at all on the fine scale of Monsieur Gilles though, and I was invited to view an exhibit at the Morwen Gallery."

"I'm interested in art, as well. I studied art history at Lady Matilda's College at Oxford." She studied him carefully, hoping to read something in his eyes, some hint of deception. He just smiled back, smooth and polite, unreadable. Blast him. But he had mentioned the Morwen Gallery, and Maddie remembered it was the place where Sophie and the other graduates would be displaying some of their work. "Will you be at the Morwen tomorrow, then?"

"I hope to be, certainly. I understand there are some extraordinary works to be viewed there."

"Oh, yes. Some of them are from my friend Sophie's professor, who sadly died recently." Maddie gestured toward Sophie, who was dancing at the other end of the floor. Sophie laughed at her escort's jokes, but she seemed preoccupied. Sophie waved back, her brow arching in question.

"Your friend studied with Professor Overton?" he asked, his tone bored. Too bored?

"You've heard of him? Oh, of course you would, if you deal in art."

"They say he has an—interesting eye, a good instinct for finding the true artists among his pupils. Your friend must be talented."

"She is, very much." She gave him a wary smile. "How did you become interested in art, Mr. Albrecht?"

A tiny frown touched his lips; his glance flickered

away. Maddie felt her cheeks turn warm as she wondered if she had said something wrong, pushed too hard. Her natural English reserve always left her when she was with her friends, making her forget there was sometimes a purpose to watching her words. But then he smiled and twirled her again in a light, graceful arc.

"It's bred in me," he said. "My grandfather and my father were both collectors, in a small way. They were businessmen in Vienna, not wealthy, but they both had an excellent eye and a knack for knowing what styles would one day be sought-after before they were famous."

"Such as Impressionists?"

"My grandfather did have a fondness for Renoir. He had a small portrait of a girl trying on a hat. When I was a child, I would stare at her for hours, utterly mesmerized. The expression in her eyes—what did it mean? What was she thinking? She looked rather like you."

"Like me?" Maddie said, surprised and flattered. She had never thought of herself as at all Renoir-esque.

"Yes. Smiling and serene, but with a great deal hidden underneath."

Maddie laughed. "I am not at all mysterious. But did your father also like the Impressionists?"

"Ah, every generation rebels against their elders. My father was rather more avant-garde. He liked the Abstract Expressionists. Kandinsky, Klee."

"And you?"

"I have come back to my grandfather's tastes. But I admire my father's. He was a man of rare discernment."

Maddie longed to ask more about the Renoir, the Kandinskys. Yet she feared to know the answer. There was something so sad, so secretive about this man. And so many hideous things happened in the war.

She gave him a gentle smile. "I love the Impressionists, too."

The band ended the song with a flourish, and Mr. Albrecht let go of Maddie to applaud with everyone else. She stepped back, feeling suddenly cold.

"Thank you for the dance, Herr Albrecht," she said as they made their way from the dance floor toward the bar. "And for the rescue. I don't think my poor shoes could have stood any more from that clod."

"Not at all, Miss Carlisle. I must thank you. You've brightened what threatened to be a dull evening more than I can say."

Maddie laughed. "Dull? Club 501? You have obviously never spent a blackout evening playing cribbage with my great-aunts."

He laughed, a wonderful, infectious sound that sounded a bit rusty, as if he hadn't laughed in a long time. But then again, none of them had. "I am becoming an old man, Miss Carlisle, and nightclubs don't hold the same appeal for me they once did. An ideal evening would be my own fireside and a nice pile of new books. Maybe not cribbage, though."

"I enjoy a quiet evening as well, there is always so much to read and study working for Monsieur Gilles. But being here is a real treat."

He gave an understanding nod. "London is still sadly dreary, is it not? My own city is the same. I remember how it used to be, so light and golden, so full of music."

"How very sad," Maddie answered. She had never been to Vienna, but her parents had before the war and often talked of its rare beauty, its air of sophistication and culture. "I've always dreamed of seeing Vienna. My parents did love it."

"I hope you will visit one day. It is recovering, slowly, and hopefully will regain its beauty and spirit soon." He led her to the busy bar, to the center of the crowd clamoring for drinks from Pauley. "A glass of champagne for the lady, please," he said, not even loudly, not pushing past the others, but it seemed he had a natural authority, for a glass quickly appeared.

"Nothing for yourself, Herr Albrecht?" she said, taking a sip.

"Alas, I am late for another appointment. And it looks like your friend is waiting impatiently to talk to you." He nodded toward the end of the bar where Sophie stood in a knot of her admirers. She was bouncing on the toes of her red satin shoes and waved eagerly when Maddie caught her eye. "I'm sure we will meet again soon."

"It's fated?" she said teasingly.

"And you did mention you will be at the Morwen Gallery," he answered with a laugh. He raised her free hand to his lips for a light, Continental salute. "Until then, Miss Carlisle."

As he vanished into the crowd, Sophie hurried to Maddie's side. Maddie curled her hand into a fist; it still tingled from the brush of his lips.

"Who was that?" Sophie asked.

Maddie took a long drink of her champagne. "His name is Mr. Albrecht, an art dealer of sorts."

"Really? I've never seen him before, or I'm sure I would remember him. He's like a movie star. Lucky you, dancing with such a looker!"

Maddie laughed. "He had to rescue me from *your* friend."

Sophie pulled a rueful face. "Sorry about that. Bob can be such a lout when he gets a drink in him."

"So I discovered." Maddie studied the crowd around them, which had grown thick and noisy as the night went on. She wondered what kind of art Christoph Albrecht dealt in and what really brought him to Boston. He was good at evading questions, at giving just enough information without really giving anything away. "Mr. Albrecht says he'll be at the Morwen Gallery opening. He seemed interested in your Professor Overton."

Sophie glanced away, shifting on her heeled shoes. "You don't think he could have something to do with it all, do you?"

Maddie blew out an exasperated breath. "To do with what, Soph? What's really going on here? I can't help you if I don't know absolutely everything. Are you in trouble?"

Sophie looked around quickly. "We can't talk here. Meet me before the Morwen party tomorrow? Or better yet, let's go out after we leave here. I'll tell you what I know then, but I'm afraid it's not much."

Maddie only had time to nod when the band launched into a drum roll, and a handsome, beautifully-dressed man stepped onto the stage, owning it as if he was a movie star himself. It had to be Leo, Aunt Meggie's manager. "Good evening, ladies and gentlemen, and welcome to Club 501! It's now that moment you've all been waiting for. Please welcome the stunning Lady Margaret back to her home stage!"

The curtains swept apart, and Audra's mother

appeared in a pool of silver light that made her bright hair and beaded gown sparkle. She launched into her signature song and the rest of the club just seemed to melt away into the shadows. Maddie looked around for Christoph, but he was gone.

****

He hadn't expected to see her tonight. Miss Madeline Carlisle. She was certainly a distraction he didn't need as he closed in on Emmerling at last.

Christoph stepped outside the door of Club 501 to light a cigarette. The street was a busy one, lined with restaurants and clubs, the streetlights shining down on the well-dressed, laughing crowds hurrying past. He noticed them all, every face, every lipsticked smile, every averted face under the brim of a hat. He had to see what was around him at all times; he could never relax.

Except when dancing with Miss Carlisle, looking at her smile, feeling her lithe waist under his touch.

It was interesting news, though not very welcome, that she was connected to Frank Markov and Monsieur Gilles, that she knew the art world. He doubted she had anything to do with the art smuggling, or even knew about it, not a young English aristocrat like her. But then again, appearances were often so deceptive. He had learned that hard lesson in the war. Miss Madeline Carlisle was someone to be watched closely, along with her friends. Especially the artist.

Christoph put out his cigarette and made his way to the street corner to find a taxi. He heard the steady patter of footsteps somewhere behind him, slowing when he slowed, growing faster when he increased his pace, separate from the rest of the crowd. He casually slipped one hand into his pocket, feeling the weight of the knife he carried there. When he reached the corner, he glanced back. The sidewalk was empty.

Chapter Six

"Are you sure we should be doing this, Soph?" Maddie whispered uncertainly as she followed her friend up a back staircase in the Fine Arts building at Roseline. It was the dead of night, the only light from the electric torch Sophie brought, and their footsteps seemed to echo like thunder in the emptiness. The ivy-draped buildings, so venerable and dignified in the day, looked ghostly in the dark.

It was scary, but also rather thrilling, Maddie had to admit. Like something in a detective story.

"Of course not," Sophie answered cheerfully. "But when else can we look around without anyone bothering us? Don't worry—I've been here before after hours, and I know the security guard won't pass by for at least another hour."

"I guess I shouldn't ask what you were doing here after hours?"

Sophie laughed. "I wasn't meeting boys or anything, silly. It's a good place to paint, with the whole studio empty and no one peering over my shoulder. At home, my mother worries if I stay up late. She worries about everything, really."

Maddie couldn't really blame Aunt Charli for worrying, not when her daughter was as fearless as Sophie always had been.

At the top of the stairs, they turned down a long

corridor and made their way to a doorway near the end. The air was warm and stuffy, filled with the sharp scent of turpentine and oil paints and dust. Sophie took one of the diamante-headed pins from her short, dark curls and slid it into the lock of the door. With a couple of deft twists, she clicked it open.

"Can you show me how to do that?" Maddie asked in admiration.

"Oh, sure. It's easy," Sophie answered. She led the way into the room, which seemed to be a class space. Moonlight from the tall windows fell on rows of covered easels set up in front of a model's dais, making the whole thing even more ghostly.

Maddie followed Sophie to another door half-hidden behind a screen in the corner. Sophie made short work of that lock, too, and they went into an office. A desk was cleared of everything but a lamp, but books still lined tall shelves, and there were narrow sliding racks for paintings.

"This was Professor Overton's," Sophie said. "He usually cleans out after the end of a semester, but they left these. You have to see them."

Sophie snapped on the lamp on the desk and slid a few paintings out of the narrow racks. She propped one up on the chair. "What do you think, Maddie?"

Maddie carefully examined the canvas. It was a portrait of a woman in black staring out a window, her chin in her hand, a contemplative look in her eyes. "It's excellent work. If it wasn't so bright and new, I would think it was a Degas portrait."

"But it's not. It's mine. See?" Sophie pointed out her mark, a Celtic symbol of four friends. "I always put that on the copies we worked on for class. But there's also this."

She took out two other paintings, also copies of Poussin and Hassam. But they had been subtly altered. If not for the small mark, Maddie would have been quite fooled, and she thought even Monsieur Gilles would have had his doubts.

"Someone was careful to clean everything else out," Sophie said. "Including the professor's art supplies. I found these behind that cabinet. It just seems to confirm what I suspected before, when he tried to get me to do even more copies."

Maddie frowned as she studied the works. "You think your professor was selling forged art?"

"It looks like it, doesn't it? There's something else, though."

"What's that?"

"I happened to come here one day after class to ask Professor Overton something. It was after office hours, but I heard voices coming from this room. One was Professor Crichton, but one of them had a distinctly German accent."

Maddie thought of Christoph Albrecht, the mysterious art dealer. She certainly didn't want to think ill of someone so handsome, but his appearance in Boston just at this moment did seem strange. "What were they talking about?"

Sophie frowned. "It was hard to hear, they were so muffled. They definitely sounded angry. I could only catch a few things, but one was the name Emmerling. I know I've heard that name before, he was one of the Nazis who vanished, along with a fine purloined art collection."

Maddie nodded, remembering Monsieur Gilles and

the lost Degas. "So he was smuggling art for German fugitives, using your work as cover?"

"It sure sounded like that. It would be easy enough to cover a stolen painting with a copied one to get it shipped out, and no one would question a respectable art professor. If he *was* dealing with the Germans..." Sophie broke off.

"Then maybe he paid for it with his life," Madeline whispered. The building now sounded even more quiet.

"If there's any chance I could find some of that lost art, I have to try," Sophie said. "I hoped you could help, with your job with Monsieur Gilles. When I got your postcard, I was sure of it."

Maddie nodded. She quickly told Sophie all she knew from the gallery in London, of the missing Degas last seen in a Nazi photo, and what happened to it after. She didn't mention Christoph Albrecht, though, since she didn't know what part he might be playing in the whole scheme.

"That day I heard voices in here," Sophie said, "I hid behind the screen and waited for them to come out."

"Sophie!" Maddie cried. "That could have been so dangerous if you were caught."

"I was careful! I had to find out, didn't I? Anyway, there was the professor, two men I didn't know, and the fourth was a man named Mr. Perry, who works at the Morwen Gallery."

"Where your graduation show party is going to be?"

"Exactly. I thought maybe we could have a little look around while we're there."

Maddie examined the paintings in front of her. "I think that would be a very good idea..."

Chapter Seven

At first, Maddie had no idea what to say as the cab sped on its silent way through the brightly-lit city, past towering office buildings and rows of townhouses, restaurants, and clubs. Christoph sat so close to her on the cracked leather seat, so close she could feel his warmth, smell the clean, lemony scent of his cologne, and it made her want to giggle and cry all at the same time.

Don't be such a ninny, she told herself sternly. He was sophisticated man, and she—sometimes she didn't even know who she was any longer. She just knew she didn't want the ride to end.

"Your friends seem—very lively," he said.

Maddie laughed. "Oh, yes! They always have been, ever since we were children. I've missed them so much."

"Yet you didn't want to go dancing?"

"Sophie was right—I am an old English matron now, fit only for a cocoa and my knitting needles at such an hour," she said lightly, desperately hoping he wouldn't think that was true. For some reason, she wanted him to believe her to be beautiful and fascinating and intelligent, though how could that be so after all those Viennese ladies he must know?

Christoph laughed, a rough, smoky sound she

longed to hear more of. "Now, why don't I believe that?"

"Oh, no, it's quite true. I'm an Oxford bluestocking, you know."

"Now that I cannot agree with, I fear."

Maddie dared peek up at him then and wished she had not. She was too lost in his eyes, those pale blue depths like an Alpine lake. Like drowning in endless icy waves that pulled her deeper and deeper. She felt like someone in one of the racy French novels some of the girls at Oxford had loved so much, caught in moments that felt out of time, sparkling, delicate, perfect. His expression changed as he looked at her, darkened.

She was drawn closer to him, unable to turn away, as though invisible, unbreakable bonds tied them together. As if in a hazy, warm dream, she felt his arms come around her, drawing her so close nothing could come between them. Maddie found herself longing to seize the moment, to make it her own and never forget it.

She looped her arms around his neck and closed her eyes, inhaling the warm scent of him, of fresh air, clean linen, faint lemon-y cologne, of Christoph himself. It made her feel dizzy, giddy, like too much champagne.

She gently touched his cheek. He moaned, a low, hoarse sound, and his lips claimed hers at last. She met his kiss with everything she had, all the emotion locked away inside of her. It wasn't a gentle kiss, as surely first kisses usually were, but one filled with heat, desperation, need. She wanted it to go on and on, forever.

A screeching sound nearby broke into Maddie's dream, and she pulled back from his embrace, hot and cold all at the same time. Flustered and panicked, and full of a strange, bursting—joy. Had she just *kissed* this man, this mysterious man? Where had such a fantastical thing come from?

She stared up at him in astonishment. He looked just as shocked as she did, a dull red flush over his sharp cheekbones. His eyes closed, and he shook his head, an appalled expression spreading over his face. She was scared he was about to apologize, and she knew she couldn't stand that. Couldn't bear knowing he though the kiss was a mistake.

Maybe it *was* a mistake. No, scratch that—it definitely *was*. But she wanted to hug the memory of it closer just a little longer.

She turned her head desperately and saw that they were at her stop. "This is me!" she chirped, in a ridiculously cheery voice. "Thanks ever so for the ride. Good night." And she hopped out before he could say anything, even though she glimpsed his hand reaching for her.

She didn't stop until she had run up the stairs, slammed the door behind her, and locked it. Her heart pounded so loudly she was sure everyone else on the block could hear it. So she threw herself down on her bed, buried her head in her pillow, and screamed with delight and embarrassment and fear at her own feelings.

Yet in the morning things did *not* seem any clearer. The headlines on the Society page of the morning paper screamed in large black letters that Professor Crichton, "eminent art teacher and scion of old Boston family" had been caught having an affair—with Sophie!

"Oh, Sophie," Maddie whispered. "What's been going on here?"

Chapter Eight

"My father is driving me mad!" Audra muttered. Maddie, trying to zip up the slippery black fabric of the evening gown her friend was trying on, had to make Audra stand still for a minute. "We had the worst fight ever last night. I told him I was moving out."

Maddie was shocked. She knew her friend had her conflicts with her mother, since Aunt Meggie was always so busy, but Uncle Harry had always seemed like the most doting of fathers. This shopping trip to New York, meant to let them all spend time together and to get Sophie over the scurrilous rumors of her affair, didn't appear to be working. "You didn't."

Audra tilted up her chin, her movie star pretty face filled with defiance—and fear. "I did."

Maddie shook her head. She did understand—her own parents often drove her mad, always so worried and hovering, especially since the war. But she loved them with all her heart and couldn't imagine being apart from them for long. It would be too frightening. She finished zipping up the dress and stepped back. The gilt and cream dressing room at Bergdorf's was a long way from the shabby splendor of her parents' townhouse, and she suddenly missed it very much.

"Well, at least you *look* beautiful, Audra. This dress is perfect for you."

Audra did a little twirl, the fabric shimmering

around her. Maddie picked up the pile of clothes draped over the velvet chaise, sorting through the lovely assortment of satin and lace. She held up one dress, a rose-pink silk, and wondered frivolously what Christoph might think of it if she wore it. Would he kiss her again? Did she want him to? "So what are you going to do about Uncle Harry?"

"I don't know," Audra answered with a sigh. "But something has to give or one of us is going to end up saying something unforgivable. I love him, but he has to let go."

"You can't break with him entirely! He loves you so much, just as you love him."

"I know." Audra smoothed her hand down the skirt of the dress, her eyes downcast. "I—I think I've misjudged my mother, though. For twelve whole years." Her voice sounded thick with tears, which was not at all like Audra, who charged confidently through life. It is nice, isn't it?"

Maddie hurried to give her a hug. She remembered once hearing her mother and her Aunt Jessica, who had been Meggie's best friend since school days, talk about how they worried that Meggie's busy career kept her from her daughter. Maddie had dismissed it at the time; Audra always seemed so happy. But maybe they had been right. "Oh, Audra, I'm so sorry. But surely this is good for you and Aunt Meggie?" She had a sudden thought, a memory of how a change of scene could be so helpful sometimes. "When I go home, why don't you come to London for a bit? Stay with me? I'm working a lot at the gallery, but there's plenty of time for fun, nightclubs, and the theaters. It's a brilliant idea!"

And maybe having her friend close would help her

forget, too, once she knew she wouldn't see Christoph Albrecht anymore.

Audra sniffled. "It *would* be fun. I haven't been to Europe in ages." She pulled back to look at Maddie with wide eyes. "But are *you* okay, Maddie? You seem awfully preoccupied today."

"Oh, no, I'm fine. Just not sleeping much." She wasn't quite ready to talk about Christoph, his kiss and her suspicions about the stolen paintings, not yet, not even to Audra. She picked up the pink dress again. "What do you think about this one? It's such a treat to actually have a choice in clothes again!"

"It's a nice color, but I like this one better." Audra picked up a grass-green frock sprinkled with white polka dots. "More va-va-voom, you know?"

"I don't think I've ever worn anything—va-va-voom," Maddie said with a laugh. "I do like it, though."

There was a sudden knock on the dressing room door. "Hey, what's going on in there?" Iris called. "Sophie and I want to see the dress!"

"In a minute, Miss Bossy Pants!" Audra answered. She gave Maddie a worryingly weak smile. "Maybe I'll take you up on that London thing, Maddie. I could use a break from Boston."

Maddie slid on the green dress over her slip and pretended to be occupied with it in the mirror. But in her mind all she could think about was how much she would miss this little Boston adventure once it was over. And it would be over all too soon.

****

"Oh, come on! We don't have much time." Sophie ran up the grand stone steps to the front doors of the Metropolitan Museum, dodging tourists and souvenir sellers. Over lunch, she had persuaded them to take a later train back to Boston so she could examine the new Poussin exhibit. Maybe she just didn't want to go back to Boston to face the gossip, but for the moment she seemed happy enough.

The grand entrance hall of the museum was crowded, people swirling between the marble pillars to the Egyptian wing or up the grand staircase toward the European paintings. After leaving their shopping bags at the coat-check, Sophie disappeared immediately, and Audra and Iris wandered up the stairs to look at some Renoirs. Maddie took advantage of the time to try and find Monsieur Gilles' friend, the Mr. Sanders who worked at the Met and had been on the trail of the Emmerling paintings. Surely he would be able to tell her something.

She found a half-hidden door at the back of one of the Grecian galleries marked "Curators Only," and slipped through it. A secretary at a desk just inside glanced up with a suspicious frown.

"Can I help you?" she said, peering over the top of her spectacles.

Maddie smiled, putting on the fine, cool British manners she had learned from her mother. "I'm so sorry to interrupt your work, but I am Madeline Carlisle. I work for Monsieur Gilles in London. He said I should look for one of his friends while I'm in New York, a Mr. Sanders. I have so much to learn about galleries and museums, you see, and the Met is surely the finest place in the world for that."

The woman relaxed a bit. "Monsieur Gilles, you say? We haven't seen him here in some time. I hope he is well."

"Very well. Very busy."

"Aren't we all these days? I'm afraid Mr. Sanders is out this week, taking care of some personal matters, but I will tell him you called."

Personal matters? Maddie thought that sounded rather suspicious, considering all that was happening around the Emmerling paintings just then. It was obvious the secretary expected her to leave now, but Maddie was reluctant to do that just yet. The offices looked most intriguing, narrow rows of cabinets stretching in every direction that surely held the most delectable artworks. She turned and strolled slowly toward the door, but when the secretary looked away to answer a phone Maddie ducked behind a row of those shelves.

She followed the aisles, the whole room dimly lit from fixtures high overhead, the windows shuttered to shield the works from sunlight. She glimpsed a couple of studios where restorers labored at their easels, but other than that the rooms were empty and silent.

Until she came to the end of the row and suddenly heard the hum of voices coming from behind a half-open door. The door was labeled M. Sanders, and she wondered if the secretary had been fibbing, if Monsieur Gilles' friend was in after all. Or maybe the men, she could hear three of them, were just using the empty office.

One of the voices was familiar, Mr. Perry from the Morwen Gallery.

"...has to be now. We can't wait any longer."

"We don't know if they're the right ones. How can you trust this person?"

"Because I know him. I met him at Neuchwanstein,

and I know he wants them back just as we do."

"But what if..."

Maddie's shoe suddenly hit a heavy box on the floor as she tried to move closer, knocking it into the wall and making a clatter that made her jump, so intent was she on the men in the office. They went silent, and she instinctively spun around and fled back the way she came.

She found another doorway, far from the watchful secretary, and stumbled out into the crowded museum just as she heard Mr. Perry call out, "Wait! Please!" She ducked into a tour making their way through the maze of Grecian vases and marble goddesses and ran up the stairs to look for her friends. Something strange was going on there, and she didn't want to get trapped in those quiet, hidden offices until she knew more about what it was.

She found Audra and Iris in the Impressionist galleries, but no Sophie. When they went in search of her, they found her on a leather couch in the ladies' lounge on the second floor, all alone, her face pale beneath the straw edge of her hat. In her gloved hand, she clutched a balled-up paper.

Audra knelt down beside her and said gently, "Soph, we need to go now, if we're going to make our train at Penn Station."

"Are you ill?" Iris asked, taking out a handkerchief to pass Sophie.

Sophie blinked up at them, almost as if she was coming awake from a strange dream. Maddie knew the feeling very well. She wasn't at all sure the scene in the office had really happened.

"Yes, yes," Sophie said, jumping up.

"Is something amiss?" Maddie asked. She tried to put her arm around Sophie but was shaken off.

"No, of course not. I'm ready. We should go," Sophie gasped, rushing out of the lounge.

Maddie and others hurried behind her, trying to keep up. As they came to the foot of the stairs, Maddie was sure she felt someone watching her, but when she looked back there was only the crowd of tourists.

****

Maddie was sure she would collapse at any moment as she stumbled into her borrowed Boston bedroom late that night. The long day of trains, shopping, and museums had finally caught up with her, and her head was spinning trying to process it all.

She kicked off her shoes and tossed her hat on the bed, the events of the day turning over in her mind. She was terribly worried about Sophie's strange behavior; her friend had hardly spoken on the train home. And then there were the men in the Met offices.

As she unbuttoned her suit jacket, she noticed the mail left on the bedside table. A letter from her mother, a catalog from Bendel's—and a note without a stamp, surely hand-delivered. Curious, she tore it open.

Miss Carlisle, would you do me the honor of taking tea with me tomorrow at the Palm Court at the Park Plaza? I feel we have much to discuss, and I have much to explain. I hope you had an interesting day in New York. Sincerely, C. Albrecht.

Maddie found herself smiling to see that name and quickly bit her lip to make herself stop. She shouldn't be mooning over a man who obviously was involved in something rather mysterious and possibly quite dangerous, but she couldn't seem to help it. Tea at the

Park Plaza. The perfect opportunity to get some answers.

Chapter Nine

"I'm here to meet a Mr. Albrecht," Maddie said, trying not to fidget with her hat and purse. The Palm Court at the swanky Park Plaza hotel was so very elegant, it was hard not to gawp like a country schoolgirl at the stained glass ceiling, the gilded chairs, the fashionable hats. She was very glad of the New York shopping trip now; her rationed English suits would never have done.

The maître d', who matched the surroundings with his tall, spare elegance and dark suit, studied her for a moment before he looked down at his open reservation book. "Ah, yes. Two for tea. Charles, please show the lady to Mr. Albrecht's table. The gentleman has not yet arrived."

Maddie followed the waiter past groups of ladies in chic Dior suits whispering over their dainty teacups, past the murmuring fountain and the chamber orchestra playing quietly in the corner. He led her to a table tucked in a lovely little alcove, beautifully quiet, where she could watch the room without feeling on display herself.

"I'll fetch the tea menu right away, miss," the waiter said as he held out her gilt and brocade chair. "Perhaps you would care for a champagne while you wait?"

Champagne—at tea. Maddie gave a blissful sigh.

That was what she needed, a bit of liquid courage. "That would be lovely, thank you."

As she sipped at the delightful, golden bubbles, she thought over what she had seen in New York. But what she was going to do about it—that she didn't know yet.

She still hadn't decided when Christoph arrived a few minutes later, so elegant and golden in his charcoal gray suit, a felt hat and gloves in his hand and a pink rosebud in his buttonhole. He looked like he stepped from a movie.

"I'm so sorry for my tardiness," he said, greeting her with a very Continental double-cheek kiss.

"Not at all. I was a bit early," she answered, charmed despite her worries. He always had that effect, blast him. "All the better to savor this lovely glass of champagne. So very decadent."

He sat down across from her, nodding at the waiter. "You are looking most charming today."

"Thank you. I went shopping with my friends in New York yesterday. But I think you might already know that."

His smile didn't even waver. The waiter appeared at their tableside with pots of tea and a trolley of dainty sandwiches and tiny cakes. "Why would I know that?" he said once they were alone again.

"I saw your friend Mr. Perry from the Morwen Gallery in the offices at the Met. I thought perhaps he might have mentioned it."

Christoph took a sip of his tea, and Maddie wondered if he was buying himself a moment. "Surely there is nothing strange about an art dealer being at an art museum, Madeline."

"No. But his companions at the museum seemed

decidedly odd, as if they didn't want to be seen." The waiter came back to hear their selections from the tea cart, and when he left Maddie sat back in her chair with a smile of her own. "Please, Christoph. I know that you aren't just here to buy art. You told me your family had lost much in the war, as so many others have. Does your work here involve recovering some stolen art?"

His smile turned to a small grimace. "Of course you would remember that."

"It's a difficult thing to forget, especially since I work in much the same field. If I can help in any way, I want to, very much. Monsieur Gilles in London suspected that some pieces were passing through Boston for a certain Herr Emmerling, and he's terribly afraid they might vanish forever. If that's what you think as well..."

"What if I'm the one stealing the art?" he said, his tone completely neutral, his smile returning. "I am Austrian, after all. Practically German."

Maddie studied him carefully, looking into the icy blue of his eyes. "That's not what Mr. Perry said, and one of the chief curators at the museum vouched for him."

"So you spoke to George."

"Saw him. When I was—taking a little look around the museum. I remembered him from the Morwen."

"Taking a look someplace besides the public galleries?"

Maddie shrugged. "You have to look deeper if you want to find the really interesting things in life."

"I would certainly agree." He passed a plate of cucumber sandwiches. "What did George say?"

"I didn't talk to him. He seemed quite

preoccupied."

"I'm sure he was. You wouldn't happen to work for your English Foreign Office, would you? They seem to be reaching their tentacles into many matters lately." He offered some of the pink-iced petit fours.

"Of course not. My father would never have let me go into politics, and I would be rubbish at it anyway." She took a nibble of one of the cakes. "Oh, heavens, but that is delicious. Real sugar! And no, Christoph, no politics—I just care about the art and about justice. Please tell me what's really happening. Let me help, if I can. I'd never forgive myself if I didn't."

Christoph hesitated, but finally he nodded. "You do know most of it. I'm here looking for a man named Emmerling, as you know, who used his position as a gauleiter in Austria to seize artworks. He escaped the Allied authorities after the war, and his substantial new art collection vanished with him. Mostly Impressionists, from the daughter of a distinguished Jewish dealer. We've had little luck tracing him—until recently."

"Who is we?"

"A group of concerned art lovers. Your Monsieur Gilles would vouch for us if you care to cable him. He was most helpful in finding the winding path of a certain Degas. Some of the works went through New York, hence the Met connection, bound for South America. George rescued a few, with the help of a curator named Sanders at the museum."

"But not all? Not the Degas?"

"Not all." Christoph frowned. "We found out a few shipments had arrived here in Boston, but there the trail has gone rather cold. There were suspicions some of the college faculty here were in on the scheme. I'm here to trace them, and hopefully Emmerling as well. There are many who would rejoice to see him brought to justice."

"I'm sure." Maddie nibbled at another cake, thinking over everything that had happened. Sophie's professor and his shady paintings; the museum back corridors; Nazis creeping through the Boston docks, hiding artworks. It all sounded like a movie, and yet here she was in the middle of it. "I think I may be able to help you."

"In what way?"

"My friend who was the student of Professor Overton. She is indeed very talented, and it seems the professor might have been using that talent to his own ends." And whatever those ends were might have led to the Crichton rumors. Maddie quickly told him what Sophie had shown her, the copied paintings left in the office, the possibility they had been used to either cover up stolen paintings or substitute for them. She chose not to mention Sophie's strange behavior at the museum.

Christoph leaned closer, his eyes narrowed. "Most interesting. We have long suspected the man was more than a mere art teacher, and his vanishing seemed to prove that, but our searches turned up little. So your friend Miss Noble thinks she's found a clue there?"

"Yes, in her own paintings. Though she herself would *never* have knowingly taken part in such a thing."

"I'm sure. Yes. The professor was mentioned a few times by our contact here, but then that trail went rather cold."

"I could show you the paintings, if they haven't been moved again. Sophie's graduation is tomorrow, there will be so many people wandering the campus that two others won't be noticed. There's a party afterward, too, at Club 501."

"Very clever, Madeline. Are you sure you don't work for the Foreign Office?"

Maddie laughed. "Too much trouble, with such long hours. If the art world is so dangerous, I can't even imagine spy work."

His smile faded. "Madeline. We laugh now, but this is indeed dangerous. You should stand back once we find the paintings."

Maddie waved off his warnings. "Please, Christoph. If a war criminal and his purloined art escape when I could have helped in any way, I would never forgive myself. Everything I learned, everything I care about, wouldn't matter at all. Now, tell me more, if you can..."

He couldn't, or wouldn't, and the talk soon turned to more inconsequential things, favorite artists, Viennese pastries. When they left the Park Plaza, it was raining, a fine, gray drizzle that made her think of London. They stood beneath the dark green awning to wait for a taxi.

"Madeline," Christoph said solemnly as he started to hand her into the car. "Please, be most careful. Perhaps it would be best if you went back to London."

Maddie smiled up at him. "But I can't, not until after the graduation. Thank you for tea, Christoph, it was lovely. I hope we can talk again soon."

As the taxi sped away, she glanced out the back window to see him watching her go with a frown on his handsome face. Did he want to protect her, or was he hiding something? Either way, she was determined to find out, very soon.

Chapter Ten

"Ellen   Lundgren.   Victoria   Mortimer.   Jane
Morrison."

Dear heavens, but who knew there were so many
names to be called for a graduation? They hadn't come
anywhere near Sophie's turn yet. Maddie checked her
watch and glanced at the bunting-draped stage at the
end of the faux-Elizabethan, dark paneled grand hall
with its stained glass windows and coats of arms on the
walls. She had never been to a graduation before—
when she finished at Lady Matilda's, she went to Paris
for a short art history conference. It all seemed just as
full of slow pomp as a royal court event, a presentation
drawing room, or garden party, and just as dull.

She craned her neck trying to find Sophie in the
line of robed graduates and couldn't see her. Behind
her, her aunts were whispering and giggling like
teenagers, and she rather suspected one of them had
sneaked in a flask. She studied the crowd around them,
but she didn't really see the stylish hats and silk ties.
She kept thinking about New York, the lost paintings,
and Sophie's strange behavior.

She glanced at the faces of the row of professors at
the back of the stage, all of them with bland smiles on
their faces. Would Professor Overton have been there if
he hadn't vanished? Or would he have been somewhere
in hiding, scared after he realized his art forgery

schemes involved murderous Nazis? The thought of it all seemed so strange amid this staid, quiet place, almost surreal.

Just as her own life had become. Once Boston was all over, what would it be like to return to her ordinary days in London? Typing up catalog copy and serving champagne to art buyers. Maybe she would like the quiet order of that life again. Or maybe she would miss the excitement of chasing after stolen art, even in a small way.

She would definitely miss Christoph. Maddie frowned as she thought of him. He was too handsome for any woman's peace of mind, and too mysterious. Like a man in a suspenseful novel. She wished she could read him as easily as that.

"Sophie Noble."

The sudden sound of Sophie's name being announced startled her out of her daydreams, and she leaped up to applaud. Sophie grinned brightly as she held up the scroll of her diploma, her own strange preoccupation vanished for a moment and the old, puckish Sophie shining through. It was a wonderful moment, full of the all the years of warm, summertime friendship, all the hard work they had given to building their futures.

But Noble was in the middle of the alphabet, and there were still several black-robed graduates to sit through. Once it was all over, they hurried over to hug Sophie and shout out their congratulations.

Maddie stepped back to let Sophie's parents chat with her, and she bumped into another family. As she laughed and apologized, she suddenly glimpsed a new face in the crowd. A man, taller than everyone around him and broad-shouldered, with granite-hewn features and a fringe of dark blond hair over his brow. His features were heavily lined, grayish under a suntan. He was dressed up like the others, in a well-cut gray suit and dark red tie, but he didn't seem to be talking to anyone.

Maddie was sure she had seen him before, but for a moment her thoughts were jumbled, and she couldn't remember. Then it struck her like the shock of a lightning bolt. She last saw it in black and white, in a grainy photograph in Monsieur Gilles's catalog. In that photo, he had looked rather different than now, he had looked young, strong, and arrogant in his Nazi uniform as he studied rows of stolen art.

It was Hans Emmerling. She was sure of it.

Feeling frozen with uncertainty and shock, she glanced around, surprised to see that everything was going on just as before. Families laughed and hugged, and their voices were still loud. She couldn't see Christoph or anyone who could help her. Even Sophie and the others had vanished into the crowd.

When she turned to look again, she only caught a glimpse of his gray-clad back vanishing into the knots of people. She knew she couldn't lose him, and as there was no one else to help her, she had to find out where he was going on her own.

She took off after him as fast as she could, silently cursing her new heeled shoes. She dodged around families in the hall and professors on the winding stairs, trying to keep him in sight. The crowds were soon left behind for silent hallways. At the landing that led to the art classrooms, she saw him take a key from his pocket.

Maddie knew, even in the rush of her excitement,

that it would be foolish in the extreme to follow a Nazi into an empty classroom. She was impulsive, but she hoped she wasn't stupid. She didn't even have a weapon unless she counted those silly shoes. She slipped behind a cabinet in the corridor to wait for Emmerling to come out, hoping she could follow him wherever he went next.

But he was no amateur and was careful to take a circuitous path, not easy to follow. She glimpsed him in the distance, stopping to exchange a word with someone, his German-accented voice floating to her on the wind, though she couldn't make out most of the words.

"...tonight. At the docks. Aurora," the other man said. Then the two men continued on their way together.

To her shock, she realized she knew the other man. It was Jim, the tall, clumsy waiter from Club 501—and he appeared to know Emmerling rather well.

****

"And you're sure it was Emmerling?" Christoph's voice was low and urgent, barely audible over Cafe 501's band. Sophie's graduation party was already crowded when Christoph finally arrived, the bar and dance floor packed with Sophie's college friends as well as fans of Aunt Meggie's. Maddie felt like she had been fidgeting impatiently waiting for hours, though she knew in reality he arrived even earlier than he said he would.

When he stepped into the room, looking movie-star handsome in his dinner jacket, she had immediately grabbed his arm and pulled him to the quiet end of the bar to tell him what she saw at the graduation. His frown deepened as her story went on, but he didn't interrupt.

"I think so," she answered. "I've only seen him in a photo, and he seems to have aged fifty years since then. But he did speak with a German accent, and who else would be breaking into Professor Overton's office?"

"And you recognized the man he met?"

"I saw him here at 501, a waiter. He's not here now. I think he only worked here for a very short time."

"Tell me again what they said?"

Maddie quickly repeated what she had overheard.

"And they are meeting a ship at midnight?"

"Yes, I'm afraid I only caught part of the name. The *Aurora* something."

Christoph studied the room around them, his expression unreadable. "Dance with me, Maddie."

Whatever she had been expecting him to say, it wasn't that. "Dance?"

"Yes. If someone here is watching, we should look as if we hadn't a care in the world except to enjoy ourselves."

"Oh. Of course." Maddie suddenly realized what a dreadful spy she was. She was so eager to chase down criminals and save the paintings that she would give herself away in only a moment. She glanced around the club but couldn't glimpse her friends. "Yes. Let's dance."

Christoph took her in his arms and slid them both smoothly into the swirling patterns on the dance floor, twirling her in a graceful arc. As he spun her around, she glimpsed a figure at the edge of the room, a blur in a white waiter's jacket. He carried a tray, but he wasn't headed toward the tables. He went to the back doorway, and as he glanced back over his shoulder she saw it was Jim, the so-called waiter.

"Christoph," she whispered urgently. "That's him. The man Emmerling met at the graduation."

Christoph glanced over her head as he turned her again. His smile never flickered, but he smoothly spun her through the crowd toward the door. They danced through it with never even a stumble in their steps.

Once at the empty back corridor, he grabbed her hand and dashed toward the fading footsteps she could hear in the distance. Maddie cursed the tight skirt of her new green Bergdorf's dress, and hurried to keep up. She snatched off her shoes so she could run faster. Her heart was pounding so loud in her ears it was all she could hear.

As she followed Christoph around a corner, she heard a shout and a shrill scream coming from the open door to the fire escape. When she stumbled outside, she found Christoph kneeling on the sidewalk next to a man prone on the pavement. In a startled second, she recognized him as Mr. Perry, who she had last seen at the Met. Blood ran down his leg, his pant leg torn. "Go after him—now!" he was saying, and Christoph shook his head.

She ran to their side, barely noticing the tiny pebbles that tore at her new stockings. She pulled the black kerchief from Christoph's jacket pocket and pressed it to the man's leg as he gasped and whimpered.

"You have to get to the hospital," Christoph was saying, his voice tight and low.

"There is no time, I told you! I'll get Harry to call an ambulance, but you have to go. He has the paintings now, and he's on the way to the docks to make sure they're on the ship," Mr. Perry said through his tears. "A vessel called the *Aurora Belle*. The crew are on night leave so they can load the cargo. You have to find him, get them back..."

****

Maddie had been to the docks before, of course, but only once or twice to arrive on or say good-bye to a ship. Then, it was a bustling, noisy place, full of life and color. Now, in the middle of the night, it was dark and haunted-feeling, the only sound distant shouts and water lapping against the piers. The lights of the city twinkled, so close and yet so far at the same time.

The police they had phoned from 501 hadn't yet arrived when she and Christoph left the cab at the end of the pier, and when it drove off all that silence felt like a living thing, pressing down on her.

Christoph took her hand, and the warmth of his touch made her feel better, stronger. This was something so important, correcting such a huge injustice, saving historic artworks, and she had to be brave to see it all through. To finish it.

The wind whipped around them, cold and clammy, smelling of fish and saltwater. She shivered and followed Christoph to dock where Mr. Perry said they could find the *Aurora Belle*. At first, she was sure they could never tell one vessel from another, they were all packed in so tightly in their docks, like a floating jungle that blotted out the night sky. But Christoph seemed to know where he was going. Indeed, he seemed so confident, so quietly certain, that her nervousness faded as she followed him.

Her heart was still pounding, louder in her ears than the rush of the water against the metal of the ships' hulls, and she was sure she was in a dream.

They stopped near the ship at the end of the pier, a dark hulk. In the moonlight, Maddie could just make out the painted white words—the *Aurora Belle*. She couldn't see anyone aboard, no one on the decks so high above her head. But beyond the thick, wavy glass of a porthole, she glimpsed a flicker of light.

"You should wait here," Christoph said quietly. His tone was soft, yet when Maddie looked up into his eyes, she could see the steely resolve there.

He tried to protect her again, and that made her smile. Part of her even wanted to stay, to remain safely rooted to the dock. Yet the larger part of herself, the unruly voice in her mind that had only grown louder in the last few days, pushed her ahead. She found she trusted him, and what was more she trusted herself.

"I've come this far," she said. "I would never forgive myself if I turned back now. So—how do we get aboard this thing?"

He gave her a reluctant smile. "I knew it was too much to hope you would suddenly turn prudently cautious."

"We both know this is too important for that," she answered.

"Then I'm sorry to say I think there is only one way aboard." he pointed toward a ladder snaking its way up the slate-gray hull.

Maddie grimaced. "I was rather afraid of that." She followed Christoph to the ladder and murmured a silent apology to her pretty new skirt before she tore it along a seam in order to climb. She blessed those Martha's Vineyard summers of climbing trees and swimming with her friends as she scrambled upward. She refused to look down, to give in to the anxious flutters in her stomach. There was no running away now. At the railing, she grasped the cold metal and pulled herself up and over, landing with a thud on the deck.

Christoph leaped up beside her, much more graceful than she could manage, drat him. He took her hand to pull her to her feet. "Are you hurt?"

Maddie ignored her bruised backside. "Not at all. Where to now?"

"That light we saw was this way."

They made their way along the empty deck until they found a narrow stairwell winding down to the bowels of the ship. Maddie listened carefully but could hear no sounds of human activity, no voices or echoes of music. It seemed Mr. Perry was right and the crew was on leave while the artwork was boarded. She still hardly dared breathe for fear of being discovered. She nearly tripped over a pile of paddles near a lifeboat and impulsively picked one up. The feel of the smooth, sturdy wood in her hand gave her a bit of courage, even though it wasn't much of a weapon.

At the bottom of the stairs was a corridor. It was narrow, lined with closed doors, faintly lit. There at last she heard a sound, someone snapping out brisk orders in a heavily accented voice. It came from behind one of the doors.

Christoph drew out a small handgun, and she recognized it as an M1917 service revolver from the war. He waved her to stay behind him, and she decided it would indeed be a good idea not to plunge ahead of the man with a firearm.

At the end of the corridor, a half-open doorway spilled out a triangle of light. She could hear that voice ordering crates to be moved, the scrape of wood against the floor, a banging noise, and a curse.

"There's more than you said there would be," a man with a thick Boston accent cried. "You said ten crates. This'll cost you more."

"I don't think so," a German voice answered coldly. "You are being paid most handsomely to send a few parcels to South America. One or two more can make no difference."

"This is a lot more than that! I never wanted to take these anyway. You Krauts are acting like these are the crown jewels, and that's no business for a ship like this. You'll pay more, or these crates go in the harbor like that tea back in—whenever it was."

There was another scraping noise, like a box being moved without being picked up, as if the man would indeed chuck it overboard. But a sharper, louder noise followed—s sudden gunshot.

Maddie instinctively fell back a step, clutching tighter to the paddle.

"You will honor our agreement," the other man said. "Are we now understood?"

A shout rang out, a thud, a scream. Everything seemed to happen in a blur, in a mere instant. Christoph pushed open the door and stepped into the room, his gun held level, his face cold. "Step away from that poor man, Emmerling. Your paintings are not going anywhere."

Maddie slid into the small room after Christoph, taking in the scene in one glance. The sailor huddled on the floor near a stack of flat crates, while the gray-faced man from Club 501 watched Christoph with a scowl. At first, she thought Emmerling was going to surrender.

He seemed to be lowering his weapon to the floor, a strange smile flickering over his face. Instead, he swung around and fired at the cowering sailor, but by some miracle the gun refused to go off. It only made a terrible, hollow, clicking sound, eerily loud in the small room.

Emmerling flung the empty gun at Christoph's head. Christoph instinctively ducked, and Emmerling took that split second to shove Christoph out of the way and run through the open door. He didn't seem to see Maddie there, and plowed into her shoulder. She fell back, knocking her head against the wall. As the room went blurry around her, she lashed out with the oar in her hand, finding his shoulder with a hard whack.

Emmerling tumbled to the floor, and Maddie gave him another smack to keep him down. The crack of it was frighteningly satisfying. She tried to breathe, to stay calm, but it seemed like forever before she heard the wail of sirens, heard running feet as the police rushed onto the dock.

"Herr Emmerling is definitely aboard," she told them. "You are quite late."

That was all she could say before her knees buckled and she collapsed to the deck, waves of exhaustion breaking over her as the rush of action drained away. It was much harder chasing Nazis than she would have imagined—and even more satisfying. Or it would be, she thought hazily, once she had a bit of energy back...

Chapter Twelve

Maddie could barely breathe as she watched Christoph wield a crowbar with one hand over one of the crates taken from the *Aurora Belle* and left in the dockside office where she was escorted for a restorative whiskey. The cluttered room faded around her, and all she could see was that crate, all she could feel was Christoph's hand on her arm as he steadied her. She was shaking with excitement, with hope and fear, and he was the only thing that seemed to anchor her to the earth.

"Ready?" he said, and she nodded. He stepped away from her and used the crowbar to pry off the nailed-down lid. It fell away with a sharp crack, and he threw aside a pile of straw packing.

At last, a painting emerged, its colors vivid under the faint light of the windowless room. Ballerinas, twirling onstage in a froth of pastel tulle. Mesmerized, Maddie stepped closer and saw that the colors were *too* bright, the shape of the dancers' delicate, arched arms not quite slim enough, their hairstyles a bit too modern. It was a good copy of a Degas, an excellent copy, but not really one meant to deceive.

Maddie leaned closer and saw the tiny imprint of Sophie's mark in the corner. "This is my friend Sophie's work." Cold disappointment shot through her. She had really thought they found Madame Fortin's stolen painting.

Christoph nodded. "But look at this."

He pointed at a tiny crack along the top of the canvas, and her breath caught at the sight. Christoph used a paper knife and carefully peeled away the layer of Sophie's painting, which was still fairly fresh and pliable, and revealed a layer of cardboard. Beneath that was another painting. This, she could tell in one sweeping glance, was a true Degas. The ballerinas' skirts gleamed in ethereal tulle folds in the glow of painted gaslight, their necks arched as they twirled toward an impressionistic swirl of an audience.

"I can't be sure without looking at the catalog again," she said, "but this must be Madame Fortin's lost painting, the one Monsieur Gilles is searching for. It's the same composition, the same size."

"And look at this craquillieur, the way the canvas has been cut here. Yes, I do think this is what we've been looking for." He carefully drew out the other canvases layered into the crate and found the same thing—a Monet, a Corot, a Poussin, all tucked behind copies. It was the most astonishing thing she had ever seen, and she was barely even aware of the door opening as she stared at the paintings in awe.

As the agents took over, swarming over the crates, Christoph led her from the room and into a silent hallway outside. As they stepped out onto the docks, she was surprised to find it was almost dawn, the sky turning pale gray at the edges. Their section was cordoned off, but on the other ships everything was slowly coming to life again. She shivered as a cold gust of wind swept off the water, and Christoph quickly took off his evening jacket and tucked it around her shoulders. Its warmth, the scent of it, reassured her, and she smiled up at him.

"Your friends will be missing you," he said.

"I'm sure they will." Maddie laughed as she thought of all she had to tell them now, the wild story of her night. It felt like a dream in the light of day. "Sophie will be relieved the paintings have been found. She's been distraught over what her professor did. I'm sure that must be what was bothering her at the Met."

"I'm sure the authorities will want to talk to her about him," Christoph said. He drew out a cigarette and lit it as he stared out over the harbor. The sun was rising over the skyline, all bursting yellow and orange.

"She didn't do anything wrong!"

"Of course not. But she seems very observant, not to mention talented with her paintbrush. She might have realized things about the professor others have not." He took her arm and led her along the docks to a row of shops and restaurants just opening their doors to the day. One was a diner, a yawning waitress unlocking the front doors to let in the early morning dock workers. "Let me buy you a coffee, then you should get home to rest."

"I am a bit tired," Maddie admitted, surprised to realize that she really was. The burst of energy at seeing the paintings was fading, but she was sure she wouldn't be able to sleep for hours after all that had happened. She slid into the worn leather booth across from Christoph and sighed as she sank deeper into its softness. After he ordered from the waitress, Maddie asked, "What will happen to Emmerling now?"

"He'll be thoroughly questioned, with help from the Met and the Art Institute. Then I'm sure the English and the French authorities will want their turns." The coffee arrived, hot and steaming, sending its bracing bitter scent into the air. "He will go on trial and be punished, as so many others have been. Hopefully he can lead us to some of the other lost works."

Maddie took a long sip of the coffee, thinking of Monsieur Gilles and his catalogs filled with art that had been stolen and lost. Could she do more to help find them—or would she be sent back to fetching tea and answering phones once she returned to work?

She glanced across the table at Christoph. In the morning light from the windows, he looked tired as well, his face etched in sharper lines, his hair tousled, but he was twice as handsome as ever. She suddenly realized that the thrill of the work was not all she missed once she returned to London. In fact, it wasn't even what she would miss the most. That was Christoph, talking with him, laughing with him, feeling that in him she had found someone who understood her more than anyone ever had. Yes—she would miss him very much indeed.

The thought of going back to London, of living with her parents again and bicycling to the gallery every morning, made her feel quite cold.

She took another drink of the coffee, welcoming its bracing bitter darkness. "I suppose you have more criminals to chase down now."

Christoph laughed. "A few. But first I will return to Europe to testify against Emmerling."

"Then to South America?"

"There is certainly much to be found there. Perhaps Emmerling can help us trace his associates." He reached across the table to take her hand, his fingers warm on hers. "Madeline—you must be looking forward to getting back to London."

She stared down at his hand on hers and wished that the moment could never, ever end. What was he saying? Oh, yes—London. "Oh, yes. I do miss my parents. And Audra might come visit soon."

"Monsieur Gilles sings your praises. You want to go back to work?"

"Of course." She turned her head to look out the window, unable to bear seeing his face for a moment. People streamed past toward their work, oblivious to what had just happened on that very dock. "I love working with him and all I'm learning there. Working around art is all I've ever wanted. But I hope soon I can do more than bring tea to customers and make appointments."

His fingers tightened over hers, but he seemed to hesitate before he answered. "Perhaps you might consider going on with such work in a different capacity? We might never have discovered Emmerling without your help."

"I..." A tiny bloom of hope touched her heart, warm and exciting, but she pushed it away. It would never do to get her hopes up—would it? "I must admit I have enjoyed this time here in Boston. That sounds dreadful, doesn't it! I'm sure *enjoy* isn't the right word. I'm just glad I could help in any way. It's so very important to find these works, to see men like him caught."

"Exactly so. I, too, have—enjoyed this time." He smiled, and it was like the sun coming out. She couldn't help but smile in return. "Maddie, I have never met anyone like you before. You are so extraordinary. Your spirit, your humor."

Maddie laughed. "I think I could say exactly the same about you."

"And we work well together, I think. In so many ways." He raised her hand to his lips and kissed it. "I am bad at this. I've spent so many years having to be hard, remote, to have no emotions. Since I've met you, it's all so very changed. I tried to fight these feelings, to stay away from you to keep you safe..."

"But I wouldn't let you! I am terribly stubborn that way. Surely after the war we can all admit life can't be safe, for any of us. We must stand up for what we believe in. What we want."

He looked deeply into her eyes, so deeply she was sure he could glimpse her own heart. "And what do you want, Maddie?"

You, she thought. "To help you, if I can."

"Oh, yes? Perhaps you might start by accepting this?" He reached across the table and into the pocket of the coat she wore, taking out a tiny box she had never even known was there. He opened it to reveal a sapphire ring.

Maddie gasped in surprise. "Are—are you proposing, Christoph?"

He laughed, and she had never heard such a sound from him before, so rueful and young, so full of hope. "I know of Colonel Carlisle. I doubt he would deal with me kindly if I made an indecent proposal to his daughter. Besides, I—I love you, Madeline. *Ich liebe dich*. I need you by my side now, in all things, if you will have me. I realize we haven't known each other long, it can be as lengthy an engagement as you like. I can show you my home in Vienna, or we can find a place in England. Just—promise me you will think about it. That I can hope."

Hope. It had been such a long time since the world had that, since Maddie had that. Hope for a future. But now, in the sparkle of that sky-blue sapphire, in the colors of those rescued paintings, and in Christoph's smile, she could see life again. Could see that future.

"All right, I've thought about it," she said. "And I say yes. Yes."

They laughed together, disbelieving that something so wonderful could happen in the midst of so much turmoil, and he gave her a kiss that made her toes curl. A kiss that made every danger worthwhile.

"We should wait until we get back to England, though," she said. "My mother will love to have a party to plan! And my friends will want to be bridesmaids. It's been ages since we all had such fun together!"

"Whatever you like, my darling. I have you now. That's all that matters. I know now I can do anything."

"Oh, yes." Maddie kissed his hand, admiring the way the light flashed on the ring. "Together we can most definitely do anything..."

A word about the author...

Amanda wrote her first romance at the age of sixteen—a vast historical epic starring all her friends as the characters, written secretly during algebra class (and her parents wondered why math was not her strongest subject...)

She's never since used algebra, but her books have been nominated for many awards, including the RITA Award, the Romantic Times BOOKReviews Reviewers' Choice Award, the Booksellers Best, the National Readers' Choice Award, and the Holt Medallion. She lives in Santa Fe with a poodle, a cat, a wonderful husband, and a very and far too many books and royal memorabilia collections.

When not writing or reading, she loves taking dance classes, collecting cheesy travel souvenirs, and watching the Food Network—even though she doesn't cook.

Amanda also writes as **Laurel McKee** for Grand Central Publishing, the Elizabethan Mystery Series as Amanda Carmack, and the Manor Cat Mystery Series as Eliza Casey.

Email her at amccabe7551@yahoo.com

Thank you for purchasing
this publication of The Wild Rose Press, Inc.

For questions or more information
contact us at
info@thewildrosepress.com.

The Wild Rose Press, Inc.
www.thewildrosepress.com